DISCOVERING MORGANA

WITCH OF THE FEDERATION™ BOOK 01

MICHAEL ANDERLE

LMBPN Publishing
PMB 196, 2540 South Maryland Pkwy
Las Vegas, NV 89109

Version 1.00, October 2021
Previously Published as part of the megabook *Witch of the Federation*
ebook ISBN: 978-1-68500-541-2
Print ISBN: 978-1-68500-542-9

THE DISCOVERING MORGANA TEAM

Thanks to our Beta Team

Mary Morris, John Ashmore, Nicole Emens, Robert Brooks, and Larry Omans

Thanks to our JIT Readers

Angel LaVey
Jeff Eaton
John Raisor
Larry Omans
Misty Roa
Tim Adams

If We've missed anyone, please let us know!

Editor
The Skyhunter Editing Team

To Family, Friends and
Those Who Love
To Read.
May We All Enjoy Grace
To Live The Life We Are
Called.

CHAPTER ONE

Stephanie never understood why they painted cinderblock interior walls. It always left small, concave bubbles over the surface. Maybe it was for a textured effect—anything to make the decades-old school hallway look a little more presentable on a day like that. She ran her finger over the slick, shiny white paint a second before someone rammed into her shoulder from behind and knocked her to the side.

She looked up in irritation as two guys from the other class raced down the hall, chasing each other. The teacher came out of the classroom, clapped her hands, and yelled at them. "Walk, or I'll send you right back to detention. Trust me, if that one was too exciting, I can load a very rousing, small white room with no windows into your headsets."

A kid behind her sighed. Stephanie glanced back and winced at his wild red hair and braces that almost seemed intrusive. She turned away and shoved her hands in the front pockets of her jeans as she tapped her vintage Converse up and down. Patience was something she was more familiar with than most kids, but on that particular day, she struggled to keep it together.

It was testing day—the day every kid had the opportunity to

climb inside one of the full immersion pods brought in by the government and give it their best shot for a higher education worth having. They all thought about it, but most of those students considered never made it. Unless, of course, money was no object. Then, you were sent ahead to a bright and exciting future. The rest scrambled their way through the mediocre choices left for college so they could drown in debt as they stumbled through their mediocre life. Stephanie was sure there was more to it than that—more than simply settling. But then again, what did she really know? She was a teenager.

Mrs. Abbott, the teacher, stepped out of the classroom and smiled as she tugged nonchalantly on the bottom of her blue button-up blouse in an effort to get the high lace collar off her chin. "All right, single file into the room, all the way down, and around the rows. Stop in front of your pod, and you may begin reading your instruction manual."

The students whispered excitedly to one another as they shuffled forward. Kids like Stephanie had never been inside a full immersion pod. For others like the redhead behind her, though, it seemed to be an inconvenience.

He snickered as they entered. "Leave it to the government to send outdated pods."

Stephanie ignored him, made it down the line, and stood in front of her pod. She retrieved the manual, which really was only a couple of pages long with large text. Trying not to smile too widely, she ran her gaze over the sleek black apparatus in front of her. It stood as high as her stomach, bubbled at the back, and smoothed out to a rounded point at the front. On the right was a silver handle with an arrow. On the front of it was a screen for the teacher and several flashing red lights.

The students around her chatted with excitement as the teacher browsed through the rows to see if anyone had any questions. One of the boys in the front row groaned, rolled his eyes, and raised his hand in the air. "This thing won't open. The handle is all wonky."

Mrs. Abbott held her head up and muttered under her breath. In a high-pitched tone and with an almost ghastly smile, she wandered over and tapped the book. "Did you read your instructions?"

The kid's frown transformed into tight-lipped irritation. "Of course I did."

The woman's expression remained frozen like a robot, which was probably why they called her Robot Abbott. "Okay, then. Read it again."

Stephanie lowered her head to her own book but shifted her gaze to look at him. He pouted and picked the book up again and read frantically at first before he slowed as he reached the relevant section. He pursed his lips and glanced at the handle and then back at the book. Hesitation paused his hand in mid-reach, but he continued, grabbed the handle, turned it to the left, pushed in, and turned it to the right. The door hissed slightly as it opened and raised the pod top.

He folded the instructions and tossed them on the seat before he glanced up. Quickly, Stephanie looked away so he wouldn't catch her watching him figure it out. Again, she had to force herself to hold back the grin that tugged at the sides of her lips. The kid grumbled, took hold of the handle, and hauled himself into the pod. "It's not as if someone like me will be accepted anyway. This is a waste of my time."

Stephanie forced her concentration onto the instructions in front of her. She couldn't let the naysayers and entitled kids into her psyche. The instruction manual had a different picture on the front than the one she had at home so she could prepare. From the instructions it provided to open the pod, they seemed to be exactly the same, though. She put the manual down and rubbed her hands together, stepped toward the handle, and grasped it firmly.

After a slow, deep breath, she whispered under her breath, "This is the big one. Don't screw it up."

She turned the handle left, pushed it in, and then right. The compression of the space inside hissed slightly. As she raised it, butterflies fluttered through her chest. The odor of leather fabric on the seats mixed with an odd floral scent hit her senses. *It smells like my grandmother's old car. Maybe that's a good sign. I'm gonna take it as a good sign, anyway.*

Quickly, she slid into the pod and gripped the handle. She spared one last look at everyone else entering their machines before she closed the door firmly. As it latched, small lights along the edge of the ceiling illuminated the inside in a soft glow. The screen flickered on and several buttons lit up in different colors. She knew from the booklet not to mess with any of those unless instructed to do so by the administrator.

In the silence that followed, she began to wonder if she had forgotten to do something. Suddenly, a calm female voice spoke soothingly through the pod. "Welcome, student. Are you in need of instructions?"

Stephanie released her smile and said cheerfully, "Of course."

The female voice, slightly robotic in nature, continued. "Excellent. Please lie flat on your back with your hands folded on your chest."

She glanced at the pod bed, a leather-covered foam with an indentation for a human body. A small pillow was attached where her head would go. Slowly, she lay back, crossed her ankles, and made sure she was good and comfortable. "Done."

"Excellent," the voice intoned. "I am a second generation VRZ-201 training module. I am a little older but well taken care of and will be able to help you acclimate to the training scenario. Now that you are vertical and comfortable, we will move on to the next step."

Stephanie nodded. "Right."

"For the next part of your preparation, we will administer a small injection on the left side of your neck. This will release a specialized serum that will allow my technology to speak directly to the receptors in your brain. It is one of the vital parts of the new immersion, headset-free virtual experience. Please relax."

Stephanie raised an eyebrow but closed her eyes and tried to relax. She had been subjected to a barrage of immunizations over the years with the reintroduction of certain flu strains brought by visitors from other planets. These were in addition to about six or seven specialized ones her parents had saved up for to decrease her risk of cancers and other deadly diseases. Most of them weren't required, but with the way the world had evolved in manufacturing and the increase in climate change events, you didn't stand a chance past fifty if you didn't have them. Which was mostly why they were so pricey and usually reserved for the richer families.

A slight buzz beside her left ear sounded as a small needle ejected and pierced the vein running up her neck. It whirred and a small amount of yellow liquid was injected.

"Ouch," she whispered.

The pod retracted the needle. "I'm sorry about that. For your information, there is only a six percent chance of an adverse reaction to the injection. It will dissipate from your system within eight hours."

A piece slid out above her and over her head. Small sensors rested only centimeters from her temples, across her forehead, and in a spiderweb pattern across the top of her head. "This will be able to pick up the infusion as it travels through your brain," the pod explained. "It will also document your vitals for safety purposes. Now, there are two large gloves attached to the side of the pod. Please rest your forearms on the pads and slip your hands into the gloves. Make sure your fingers are right to the tip or as far as you can go."

Stephanie moved her eyes, no longer able to turn her head. On each side were black, cushioned arm-holders with tight black gloves. Small silver wires were stitched into the fabric and traced up and down the fabric. She slipped her hand in the first one and it sucked tightly onto her hand. Smiling, she did the same with the other before she flexed her fists.

On the screen in front of her, a small line appeared and began to rise up and down in sync with the beat of her heart. Below it, other numbers were displayed that changed every few seconds. The pod dimmed the lights. "Now that you have prepped, we will wait for the detection of the serum. The average wait time is five minutes. From there, we will begin the exam."

Stephanie raised her hand up and turned it back and forth. "Groovy."

The pod beside Stephanie's shook slightly but no one could see except for Mrs. Abbott, who was distracted by the two boys who still ran up and down the hallway. Inside, Kyle—the redheaded guy from the line—grunted as he tried to get comfortable in the bed of the pod.

"This is ridiculous," he muttered. "Even the base models of the five-year-old pods had soft seats with body-adjusting cushions. This is like laying on a piece of foam."

The lights on the roof flickered on. "Welcome, student. Are you in need of instructions?"

Kyle sneered at the screens in front of him. "I guess I should since you're so old. I don't want to mess up cranking the knobs or some crazy crap like that."

The pod didn't respond to his comment. "Okay. I am a second generation VRZ-201 training module. I am a little older but well taken care of and will be able to help you acclimate to the training scenario."

He scoffed. "Are you kidding me? A 201? That was made before I was even born. I'm fairly certain my dad had one when he was my age. Great. Taking it back old-school. It's exactly like this place to not provide the state-of-the-art models."

"Please find a comfortable position in the bed, facing up with your hands on your stomach," the pod replied.

Kyle wiggled again. "Right, like there is actually a comfortable position with this thing."

He grumbled but was silenced when the needle emerged and pricked him in the neck. Offended, he clutched the spot and rubbed it. "Hey. Watch out with that thing. Did you even sanitize?"

"I'm sorry. All needles are pre-packaged and sanitized before each new student enters the pod."

Kyle frowned and rested his hands back on his stomach. "I'm shocked you even have the auto-inject. I have an old 304 model in my game room, and I call it an antique. I can't believe we have to use you for this test. No wonder the kids from the west side don't have a stinking chance of getting into this thing. I guess that's all the better for me, though."

The screen up front activated and the pod explained the information. "This will monitor your stats while you complete your exam. The headpiece that lowered and your gloves will track the serum injected into your neck."

The boy squeezed his fists open and closed. "Perfect. Rusty needles, archaic software, and a damn head clamp. I should have simply volunteered my newest pod. They could have set it all up in that thing and I would be halfway done by now."

The pod didn't respond. "Your heartbeat seems to be slightly elevated."

He blinked at the ceiling. "Because I am in a time capsule with the capabilities of an iPad from a thousand years ago."

"The iPads were used on the first pod but quickly discontinued when the technology became outdated," the AI explained.

Kyle gritted his teeth. "So I have an idiot guide through this test that also doubles as an encyclopedia of completely useless information. Perfect. This should be the most fun I've had since I broke my nose."

The pod beeped. "From your records, it seems your nose was broken on March 9th, 2114 due to a fist fight with a—"

Kyle cleared his throat and raised his voice. "I get it. You know my file. There's no need to rehash my accident. I'm sure the kid who tried to hurt me has good enough memories of what I did to him."

The AI replied, "From your records, you passed out and were taken to the hospital bay."

The kid lay there with his nostrils flared and his lips tight. "Why don't we simply sit here quietly until your slow-ass system boots up and we can start this thing?"

"Of course. When the serum begins to take effect, I will give the explanation of the process and you will be allowed to begin whenever you are ready. In case of an emergency, either call out to the pod to sound the emergency switch or remove the headset."

Kyle grumbled, "Does an emergency mean this pod is far below my standards?"

CHAPTER TWO

Stephanie settled in and stared at the ceiling as they waited for the serum to take effect. She focused on the feeling of the gloves and the tightness of the elastic material with small silver wires touched with a faint green glow. She wiggled her fingers with a grin, but when her eyes shifted to the screen that ran her physical statistics, a flutter moved in her stomach.

The opportunity to test for a prep school was something that had almost consumed her mind, at least for the last five years. She found it easier, being of high intelligence, to blend into the crowds. To achieve this, she never made waves and never really got noticed. Her clothes were plain, a few years older than most but not anything too obvious. Her parents were similar to those of the other kids she knew. They worked hard, provided a roof, food, and the necessities, but other than that, she would have to determine her future for herself.

Being in that class of society never bothered her that much, but when she heard that the rich kids had the opportunity to use full immersion pods practically their whole life at home, she was jealous. She had only ever used headgear and nothing that was the newest hi-tech. Now, she was in one of the pods and she didn't know if she would be able to get the hang of it while she took a test that could quite possibly define the rest of her life.

The voice in the pod soothed through her mind. "Your pulse has seemed to increase slightly, and your muscles have tensed. Can I do anything to make you more comfortable?"

Stephanie shook her head minutely back and forth. "No, thank you. It's my first time in a pod, that's all. Why don't you tell me about the process?"

The AI went quiet for a moment. "For this government required opportunity to be tested for a placement and possible financial assistance in a prep school, you must be checked physically as well as mentally."

She thought about all those times she'd run the mile in the lower schools. "How do you check me physically if I am lying down?"

"The system capabilities are beyond in-the-moment testing. Through your blood, circulation, heart rhythm, and approximately six hundred and eighty-nine other factors, the system can see what your physical health score will be. This includes during exercises and testing," the pod answered.

The butterflies began to tame as she thought about her last doctor's appointment. She had always been in really good shape. Encouraged, she bit the inside of her lip and tried not to let the excitement increase too dramatically. "So, there may be a chance I could be accepted? I tried to calculate it on my own, but it seemed that the odds of that happening were too low for me to figure out the number."

"There might be something wrong with your calculations. It is always at least two percent. That is the statistical norm suggested. It is also the minimum before companies are required to have government oversight."

Stephanie's heart sunk. "Not for us in the government-subsidized living arrangements."

The pod was quiet. "That is a correct statement. For those who live in government-subsidized housing, it seems numbers are closer to one in two hundred and thirty-two—"

Stephanie's eyes opened wide in hope. "That's better than I thought! Man, I imagined it would be way higher than that."

The AI finished its sentence. "Thousand."

She rolled her eyes and shook her head as a smirk moved slowly over her lips. "So, you're telling me there *is* a chance?" She laughed at her own quote, knowing that Todd would have been proud of her for being so quick.

The pod replied, "About the same as dying from a rare cobra bite."

Stephanie narrowed her eyes and pursed her lips. "Are there cobras in NorAm?"

"No."

She paused and closed her eyes before she allowed her grin to show through. She had just been cut down by a pod. That in itself would probably be the highlight of her whole time in the thing. "I think I like you."

The lights flickered in the pod. "I am not programmed to *like*. But you are very polite."

Stephanie began to think she would have been better off if she'd hung out with the pod system all those years. At least it put her at ease, which was probably the entire point of the five percent humor in the system. Those kinds of things fascinated her and had done so her whole life. The pods had been around a long time, even since before she had been born, and had become an important part of society. These days, it was almost vital considering that alternate options didn't look too exciting for her.

NorAm—long before she had been born and even before her parents were born—constituted three different countries all operating under their own rule. From what Stephanie had read, opportunities, especially in the United States, were a lot more bountiful than they had previously been. However, there was still a serious difference in the financial institutions that catered to the rich, to the middle class, and to the poor. And debt for post-high-school education was a definite unless you were lucky enough to receive a scholarship.

Prep schools worked in much the same way, but the chances of someone from the middle class or lower actually getting the financial aid to attend was nearly impossible. It was a separation of class on so many levels. Stephanie chuckled to herself and thought about all the times she had tried to talk to Todd about that. He hated it when she went on rants. He called her an old-world idealist. Which she wasn't, but she admired how people used to try to make the system better. Now, she was left with a statistical chance.

Kyle opened one eye, followed by the other, his smile now clean and brace-less. His wild red hair had been tamed and his pimples were gone, replaced by smooth skin. He looked in the mirror and winked at himself. "I should have been able to bring my personal avatar over, but hey, I like creating them so let's see what you have."

A calm voice echoed through the white room around him. "Prepare to create your avatar."

The room whizzed past him while his feet remained planted firmly in place. It stopped again with a sudden jolt to display rows and rows of clothing, weapons, and modifications of personal attributes.

He nodded. "Well, I guess this is one I can't complain about too much. At least you have the updated closet function."

"We updated approximately two hundred and forty-five days ago. Please choose your avatar's presentation. Remember, this exercise is for your assessment and we recommend one of the test preparation suits directly ahead," the voice replied in a pleasant tone.

Kyle's nose wrinkled and the creases made his freckles that much more noticeable. "Yuck. So, do I have to wear one or can I do whatever?"

The pod replied, "You can choose your personal look. Please do not linger here for too long. The test must begin shortly."

He ignored the voice as he sauntered through the racks of outfits. He walked down halfway and had already discarded the initial options. "Nope, too pink…. Ugh…that's so my parent's… Nope…nope…nope…and— Wait a minute."

The boy tapped the outfit twice and walked to stand in front of the mirror and turn from side to side. He wore what looked to be an Earth play on the Dreth battle gear. The shoulder pads were large and leather with spikes on them. The front of the armor made him look much larger than his scrawny self actually was, and the black boots also sported silver spikes.

"Sweet," he whispered and selected the hair options. "This is exactly what I need."

He tapped his preferred option twice and looked up. His red hair was now in a foot-tall mohawk with a long braid down the back. Kyle flexed his fake muscled arms in the mirror and growled. He chuckled, selected a huge sword and a Dreth laser gun from the weapons area, and clipped them to himself.

The voice spoke into the room once more. "Have you completed your avatar?"

Kyle snickered at his reflection. "Hell yeah, I did. Let's get this over with."

"Checking vitals—"

He jumped and rubbed his shoulder. "Ouch, you damned droid."

"I am not a droid," she replied automatically. "Readings have returned. Your physiology does not scan in a way that suggests pain."

His lip twitched. "It was psychomaniac."

"Indeed," the voice replied after a momentary pause. "Did you mean psychosomatic?"

"Of course." He sniffed. *There's a difference?* "Didn't you hear that word, you dumb machine?"

The AI didn't respond to his question—or his attitude, for that matter. It was not programmed nor had the capability to have its own personality. "Your physical and neurological readings are completed. You are ready to proceed to testing. Welcome to the Mandatory Audition for Enhanced NeuroSync Prep Testing. Please answer—"

Kyle waved his hand dismissively. "Yeah, yeah. Just start."

Stephanie opened her eyes and glanced around when she realized that she now stood inside a white room. A voice echoed in the space. "Prepare to create your avatar."

The room whizzed past her and she put her arms out to stabilize herself. When it stopped again, she stood in some sort of huge closet. She looked at herself in the mirror, shocked at how close they had achieved her true appearance. Even her hair was back in a braid like her mom used to do for her when she was younger.

"What do I do?"

The same calming tone spoke once more. "Please choose your avatar's presentation. Remember, this exercise is for your assessment and we recommend one of the test preparation suits directly ahead."

She focused her eyes on the selection in front of her and ran her fingers across the blue and white jumpsuits. Surprisingly, she could actually feel the fabric—it was wild. Finally, she attempted to pull the one on the end out since it was all black with what looked like 3D boxes that moved constantly on the front. It wouldn't budge, though. "How do I select it?"

"Tap the choice twice," the voice responded.

Stephanie raised an eyebrow but immediately followed the instructions. Suddenly, she no longer looked at it but actually wore it. It fit tightly like spandex, and military-style combat boots on her feet laced up her calves. She took a step back and chuckled at the way her avatar moved—almost cartoon-like but with facial shadows and the anatomically correct motions of her hips and legs. It was beyond what she'd imagined.

After a quick glance at the other things available, she decided that she would simply go with what was recommended. "It's not like I have a reason to wear a full metal suit of armor—"

"Have you completed your avatar?" the AI asked.

She shrugged. "Sure."

"Checking vitals… Your physical and neurological readings are complete. You are ready to proceed to testing."

Stephanie fisted and unfisted her avatar hands nervously. "Sweet."

The AI paused a moment before it proceeded. "Welcome to the Mandatory Audition for Enhanced NeuroSync Prep Testing. Please answer truthfully, as lies will be noted and will reduce your score. Besides standardized testing, there will be questions asked of you. These subjective question and answer sessions represent forty percent of your score. There will be an immersion test which will account for thirty percent of your score, and the core questions represent another thirty percent.

"At any time, the testing agent will be able to suggest that you be moved for consideration regardless of the score. While this does not guarantee acceptance, it means you will be reviewed for your subjective answers and possibly pass to the next stage. Good luck. There will be a period of darkness as we proceed."

She drew in a deep breath and looked at herself in the mirror. "Well, here goes nothing."

Her image faded and the darkness overtook her.

Outside the pods, everything was perfectly silent.

CHAPTER THREE

The walls were plain and darkly painted with no windows to allow light into the keycard-accessed room in the main government building for Enhanced NeuroSync Prep. It was filled with monitors and those who operated them using 3D interfaces. The screens changed and flashed constantly. When you walked into the room, you would be met with an insane barrage of technological wonder.

Around eighteen individual cubicles were spread as far apart as they could be in the space across the wide expanse of the room. They weren't separated by thin walls, but instead, used the latest sound dampening technology. No sound emitted from the space, and that helped to regulate the noise since all the engineers and programmers spent their time giving information to the students engaged in the Virtual World as well as seething in frustration. They couldn't hear a single word unless they chose to talk to each other, which wasn't really encouraged at all.

Down the center row, poised relatively close to one another, two engineer-programmers sat and talked with their students while they moved their hands to navigate the program in front of them. Aaron had been an engineer and programmer with the company for a couple of years. He liked the job but not that particular part of it. Having to actually interact with the students was often a source of enormous frustration.

He sat with a blank expression on his face and watched his current student battle the virtual Dreth pirates along with a team of other students. While almost everyone else wore training jumpsuits which were recommended, this guy had gone all out with Earth-inspired Dreth battle gear and a tall red-haired mohawk. He could tell almost immediately that the kid thought he was above everyone else and didn't need to follow the recommended course of action.

The earpiece was pressed firmly into Aaron's ear and the mic perched directly in front of his lips. "No, you can't simply shoot everyone and hope that your EI support shuts the gun down if you have friendlies targeted."

He pressed two fingers on each side of the bridge of his nose and leaned on his elbow. "No, you can't program that in the heat of battle— What kind of sim is this? A real one. Have a nice day."

He went to remove the headpiece but the kid made another smart-ass answer. Aaron slammed his palm on the desk. "What? Do you really want to know the answer to that? Or is this one of those sarcastic statements you can't seem to refrain from making?"

Aaron slapped his forehead with his palm and held his arms out to each side.

His friend, who had joined the company at the same time as him—Gene—sat beside him in his own soundproof cubicle. He finished one section of testing with his student and asked them to wait so he could prepare the rest. As he put them on hold, he glanced at his colleague. The exasperation was evident as Aaron flung his arms about and waved his hands wildly. This seemed to happen to the poor man at least once every season and it looked like it was in full swing.

Gene glanced at his computer to make sure the next section

was loading and hit the mute button on his microphone. He paused, turned, and set his hands in his lap to wait for Aaron to finish. He knew this would probably be a good story. No way could he even imagine that it would end with him calmly moving on to the next student in his queue.

Sure enough, he didn't have long to wait.

He winced as the veins in Aaron's head seemed about to explode. The engineer shook his finger and stood as he shoved his chair back. His mouth went crazy and whatever he was saying, he said it with passion. Suddenly, he very pragmatically rolled his sleeves up one at a time. Then, with anger raging across his face, he raised his right arm high into the air and slammed it down on the disconnect button. Gene flinched and chuckled.

Inside the soundproof cubicle, the irate man screamed, *"Failed!"*

Aaron, at that point, had lost every shred of patience left in his body and didn't even try not to scream. He knew the damned sound dampeners wouldn't allow him to bellow at the student anyway, and no one in the office would be able to hear him. That, however, did not stop him from pounding his hand down on the red button repeatedly until the computer sent him an error message. He backed away, panting, and plopped back in his chair to bring his hands to his face and scream into them. For a moment, he seriously considered finding the kid and beating the hell out of him.

With a loud groan, he dragged his hands down his face. The motion stretched his skin so there was a gap under each eye and his bottom lip flapped open to reveal the crooked teeth in his lower jaw. His hands still holding his face like that, Aaron's gaze shifted to his left and settled on Gene, who sat there and laughed. He swished his left hand to the side to deactivate the sound barrier between them. As soon as it dissipated, he could hear his friend's raucous laughter and the sound as his hand slapped against his black dress pants.

He spun his chair to face him, gritted his teeth, and shook his fists violently in front of him. Gene smirked and raised an eyebrow. "Eye D 10 T?"

Aaron tried, he really, really did, but as he sat there in front of his best friend, he couldn't restrain himself any longer. "He only wishes he was an idiot! That kid is probably sucking on the tit of Mom and Dad's bank account. But, of course, they most likely use a Virtual-Nanny so they don't have to deal with that festering boil on the butt of society."

Gene raised both eyebrows and Aaron continued. "You would think a parent would notice that their child was a little devil heathen sent from the depth of Tartarus to wreak hell on Earth. And that the realization would prompt them to do something like set him ablaze. Or cook him in an oven. Maybe shove a dry stake of wood through his black, hollow heart. All that would happen would be that his body crumbled and blew wistfully off in the wind. Isn't it a parent's responsibility to not unleash their spawn on the rest of the world simply so others can suffer too?"

His friend shrugged. "It might be in the by-laws. But damn, if you don't already know, misery loves company."

Aaron scoffed and folded his arms over his chest. "We all wonder what a psychopath looks like as a kid. Well, there you go. Red mohawk, idiot armor, and an attitude like he could do whatever the fuck he wanted to do. I bet he has pimples all over his nerdy-ass little face."

He paused, lowered his hands into his lap, and grumbled under his breath. Gene shook his head and raised his hands. "No, don't hold back." He wasn't even sure Aaron could or would allow himself to hear him in the rage. "Please, let it all out."

"And then—" Aaron raised one arm high and pointed at the ceiling. He flicked his blond hair out of his face. "The little bleeding canker sore had the nerve to ask me how he did!"

Gene tilted his head to the side and managed to force his lips into a straight line. "I take it you didn't approve him?"

He loved pushing his friend, who always had the most dramatic and chaotic responses to the little shit-stains who ended up on the other side of his comms. For a while there, Gene thought it was some sort of conspiracy because Aaron somehow landed all the shit-heads in the system. However, after a couple of years of doing it, he realized that seventeen and eighteen-year-old kids, especially the boys, were merely naturally dirty jock straps. Ironically, they would probably have gained something out of Aaron's temper tantrum if they had been able to actually hear it.

Plus, it usually got him to settle down and allowed him to move forward with the job of interviewing students. He merely had to get it all out of his system and as fast as he could. They were never too overloaded with their students through the day considering that they had other responsibilities too, but some of them could really put a damper on your mood. Not to mention that they learned nothing from the experience because the sound dampers essentially cut everything out that seemed derogatory or negative.

The most important thing was that they communicated with each and every student and did it thoroughly. The government didn't play around with that kind of thing. They, in their political haze, thought the system actually gave these kids an opportunity. It was more likely that the creeper on the other end of the line would end up in the prep school regardless of his insane behavior during the tests.

Aaron stopped his rant, having obviously heard Gene's question this time. He leaned forward towards his friend. "Approve him? Of course not!"

He shook his head in dismay. "That mutated radioactive rodent will probably go to school because his parents want him out of the house and are willing to pay the millions it takes. Screw that kid. He won't be one of the chosen few who get in for free."

The engineer ceased his tirade and deflated, his shoulders low and his head leaned back against the headrest of his chair. That was Gene's signal. "So, buddy, do you still have any more in you?"

Aaron replied in a whisper. "No."

Gene smiled and turned his chair to face his work station. He had his own line of students waiting on him. As he moved, though, he caught the tail end of his friend's grumble. He stopped and looked at him. "Wait, what?"

Aaron shook his head and his gaze shifted to look at the low-track lighting on the ceiling. "I said…I should tell BURT to do it."

He whirled his chair around again and glanced furtively at the room, but no one was actually watching. He hissed at Aaron. "Are you out of your damned mind?"

His friend looked at him, the anger replaced by a condescending smirk and a mischievous gleam in his eyes. The chair squeaked as he rocked back and forth and rubbed his chin. "Why not?"

Gene closed his eyes for several seconds before he exhaled a deep, exasperated breath. Why he was surprised by this response, he didn't know, but this was the last time he needed to explain it to the other man. "Because there are laws, asshole!"

Aaron opened his mouth to refute that, but Gene gestured dismissively and continued. "Plus, BURT runs the Virtual Reality Worlds—all of them. I'm not sure what would happen if you randomly asked him to sit in and do the subjective analysis. Are you?"

The other man snorted dismissively, obviously not taking his adamant speech and exhausted demeanor into account in his decision. "I've studied the system for a while now. Seriously, what do you think could possibly go that disastrously wrong with that idea? BURT barely ever hits above thirty-two percent stress load except on World Events and even then, it's only up to forty-seven percent."

Aaron looked at the ceiling and shook his finger near his lips. "Well, except that one Winters Festival, but that was a fluke."

Gene thought about it for a second. "What was that incident—oh, yeah! So, let me ask this. What happens if he goes and decides to research the shit out of the Internet? I can't truly believe that you have blocked out the time he took down Kuala Lumpur's data trunk."

His friend waved him off, his face now exhausted by the debacle. "I'll make sure the student is here in NorAm. We have plenty of pipe for the data search if it happens."

Aaron's computer dinged a reminder and he glanced at his queue. Slowly, he turned back to his station and leaned forward. His head lowered until he cradled it in both hands. "I don't know what I'll do if I have another silver-spoon-licking lizard like that last one. Because the only thing that fluttered through my mind was homicide."

He looked slowly at Gene, his face red from the blood that had rushed forward, and several pieces of his blond hair hung in his eyes. "Honest to God—whichever one you believe in—I might simply hit the red button. Like, no matter what. At the first sign that you are a rich douche bag, done."

Unwillingly, he turned his focus back to his work station. "Or, hell, I might make it so everyone gets the green button."

Gene shook his head. "Pfft. A fat lot of good that would do. The ones we green-light who are worth it don't ever get picked by the government's 'randomizing factor' anyway. Some stuffy pencil pusher up in accounting has figured out a way to get money out of the students and still be on the good side of the law."

A second beeping sounded but this time, it was on Gene's side. His head turned at the alarm and he stared at the monitor to check his work projects. "Okay, I have to get back to my queue. And if you do some crazy shit, I can't know about it. This job is all that's between me and starvation."

"That," Aaron said as he straightened and pulled his headset into his lap, "is a gross oversimplification and you playing at being a drama queen."

Gene raised his chin and scooted slowly back toward his computer. "At least I'm royalty. What does that make you, hmmmm?"

Before Aaron could respond, he restored the sound barrier over the small virtual window between them. He waved, though, and his wrist moved from side to side as he pretended to be royalty. Aaron laughed and shook his head. Gene turned away and pulled himself back to the computer to look at the different stats.

He grabbed his VR helmet and slid it down over his face. No matter how much he joked, Aaron's idea was absolutely a really good way to get yourself fired or even worse. Before he clicked the button to return to his queue, he whispered, "I hope he doesn't do anything too crazy."

Aaron, who now felt a little better, spun his chair and grabbed the front of his desk to slow himself down. He picked his VR helmet up, ready to go back in, when he saw that he had two students in his queue. He scanned each one and realized that the second was from the same testing location as the miniature Chucky. "Oh, hell no. There is no freaking way I will handle another little petulant asshole. If anything, I should give him a piece of my mind. He is lucky he got away from me before I could send him to the penalty room."

He set his helmet up and pulled his keyboard toward him. After a furtive glance around to make sure no supervisors skimmed past to look in on them, he opened a logic queue and began to type.

>>check status BURT load.

>>STATUS 22%

Aaron puffed his cheeks out and tapped his hand against the desk as his gaze shifted back and forth. He leaned back and templed his fingers as he tried to be certain that he would do something he would be willing to take the repercussions for if he was caught doing it. The sound of that little shit's laugh made him shiver. "Screw it."

He put his fingers back on the keyboard and continued to type.

>> Open Link BURT

...

...

...

>>LINK OPEN: Hello Programmer Aaron C. What can the Binary Unlimited Reality Training matrix do for you today?

>>Query BURT: Review all pertinent laws regarding Student Mandated Government Testing and report back.

>>QUERY STARTED. QUERY COMPLETE. 0.0000021% LOAD AFFECTED. TIME TO FINISH, .000043 SECONDS.

Aaron rolled his eyes and leaned back. *Does BURT always have to show off?*

He took a deep breath and focused on his screen. Cautiously, he moved the next student in the queue to the main screen and scanned the info in an effort to figure out which one the next student was in.

>>Query BURT: Can BURT handle the task of querying the student B221ZA in queue and complete all requirements of the Law related to subjective test analysis and, this is the important part, not compromise the load BURT is under while running ALL virtual worlds.

>> QUERY STARTED... ... ... QUERY COMPLETE. 0.1% LOAD AFFECTED. TIME TO FINISH 0.37 SECONDS.

Aaron narrowed his eyes and rubbed his chin. He was fairly certain he could have counted almost a second on that query.

>> BURT CAN AND WILL ACCEPT THIS TASK. TASK IN QUEUE, TASK STARTED.

He opened his mouth and then closed it and simply stared at

the screen. *Did BURT just co-opt the request from me without a formal request?*

Before he could even begin to investigate what had happened, a box popped open on his screen and began to flash. The next student had entered from the avatar area and was ready to begin.

Aaron put his helmet on and pulled up the script. "Now for the next runner up on the new game show... Your life will not change..."

He figured that as long as he didn't get a snazzy jerk, he would go home that night with a job still on the books. That was good enough for him.

Stephanie could feel her body standing there, even in her avatar, but there was nothing but blackness around her. She wondered if it was an absence of light or a switch that had simply turned off her ability to see within the world. When she thought this through, she decided it was a question for a bored night researching random things on her tablet and simply relaxed and accepted the darkness as part of the whole experience.

After a few moments, her eyes reset as a small pinprick of light appeared in the distance. She immediately squinted but stopped and laughed at herself. *No, silly, this is in your mind. You don't have to worry about your eyes adjusting in these VR pods.*

The tiny hint of illumination remained static as the minutes ticked by. In the next moment, she sat in a park. Her hands rubbed over the worn wood planks on the bench beneath her. She looked up and her senses immediately went wild as they identified all the things around her. The wind blew lightly through the leaves on the deciduous trees ahead. The faint whistle of air and crinkle of leaves made her think of a time when she had sat with her father outside one of his jobs in the richer area of town. The trees in the yard had whipped back and forth, something she didn't see in the government-housing area they lived in.

She could almost see the path of the breeze as it whipped around the base of the tree. The bark was dark and crumbling, loosely attached as it wound around the knobby knots with deep recesses within. The wind moved across the grass and fluttered each single perfectly groomed blade until it reached the bench. Stephanie giggled as it teased up her body and whipped through her hair as if it were alive and tried to introduce itself to her.

With her arm resting on the back of the bench, she turned, and her eyes glistened under the almost utopian cerulean sky. Small white nebulas danced across it, and the sun burned brightly overhead although the temperature on her skin was perfect. Still, it seemed surreal to her although it was essentially a place she was familiar with. It was her world—Earth, a place quiet and complete, where she would love to visit on a regular basis. Parks like the one she sat in still existed, but they were usually tucked tightly in the center or the immediate surroundings of the large cities.

While parks had been built near her government-subsidized living arrangement, over the years, they had fallen into ruin. The play area was rusted and dirty, and when the parents weren't there during the daytime to watch their children closely, the gangs gathered in the dusk and planned their next iniquitous act, whatever that might be.

She closed her eyes for a moment and tilted her head toward the ball of light in the sky. The simulation was so real, she could actually feel the rays of light permeate her often pale skin.

"Hello." A soft male voice spoke in her ears.

Stephanie's eyes opened wide and she set one hand down on the bench and turned from side to side. Her gaze drifted all around before she stilled nervously and placed her hands in her lap. Slowly, she stood and began to walk. She wound between the trees and ran her hands along the bark and down to the bushes.

Each individual leaf eased across her palm, warm like the sun. She knew they didn't really exist, but they seemed as real as they would if she were out of the pod.

The voice spoke again, and she straightened when she finally realized it was not a physical person but a voice in the pod. "You have finished the physical and mental congruence testing. It is time for you to take the standardized testing. How would you like the classroom to look?"

Stephanie bit her bottom lip and grinned. "Can I see Meligorn?"

CHAPTER FOUR

"Of course," the voice answered and helped to encourage the calm and warm feeling in Stephanie's stomach.

The scene around her began to change as the bushes and trees almost seemed to melt away to be replaced by the beautiful and exotic land of Meligorn. Her eyes sparkled and she touched her hand to her chest as a small, tree-like plant appeared in place of the large, thick trunk of the Earth tree. Its small branches seemed incredibly fragile while the lines and divots on its slender trunk looked weather-worn. The leaves erupted like a blooming flower and brightened her senses with deep purples and greens.

Her gaze fluttered to the horizon in the distance that no longer burst with the color of the ocean. Instead, it hummed in a translucent purple with two faint moons in the distance. What had been a line of forest in the park quickly shifted, grew larger, and morphed into large, looming mountains. The color across the horizon of the sky changed from early afternoon to the vaguely purple hue of early evening in Meligorn.

She spun in a full circle to absorb the stark contrast of beauty that erupted all around her. Soon, her clothes rippled as the soft green grasses of the park changed to a meadow. To her right, clear green water, crystalline and sparkling, reflected the light. Some sort of Meligornian creature with eight legs hopped off a blue pad and splashed quietly into the water. Her gaze trailed to the sky once more at the loud squawk as something flew over her head.

Enthralled, she studied the bird-like creature with a vast wingspan. It had the face and body shape of a phoenix, but instead of a burning red, its feathers were a multitude of alternating hues that seemed to shimmer and change with the light of their star.

She clapped her hands to her mouth and then slapped them down on her thighs. Her face broke into a prodigious smile. "Oh, my God, I'm on Meligorn! I can't believe it. The pictures are nowhere near as beautiful as it is in person."

Delighted, she dropped onto the ground and sat with her legs to the side. She traced her hand softly over the tips of the grasses that felt almost silky soft. While they were a rich bluish-green in color, they could almost pass for winter rye on her planet.

Stephanie sat there for several moments and allowed the delicacy and allure of the landscape around her to seep deeper and deeper into her mind. She didn't want to forget a moment of it. Not a splash of color, not a whisper of the softened breeze that blew against the back of her neck, and not even an interval of sound from the creatures so foreign but so fascinating to her.

A tear pooled at the corner of her eye and she wiped it away before it could trail down her cheek. She feared that if one fell, it would open the floodgates. Even though she spent her days hoping beyond hope that she would one day walk the planet of magic, she knew that moment was the closest she would get to Meligorn in her life. Of course, she could figure out a way to scheme and sneak to hitch a ride to the planet. But she had no idea how to be that kind of person. Or how to win the lottery—the approval she needed to learn in the prep schools.

She leaned back and put her feet out in front of her as she

stared at the sky. Taking in one deep breath after another, she pushed the feeling of sadness away and saved it for another time. She pursed her lips and sat up again, plopped her hands into her lap, and drew her shoulders back to demonstrate her normal hopeful veracity. Her gaze shifted all around as she thought about her unexpected time on Meligorn.

Although the person who had brought her there no longer spoke, she could feel his presence in her head and all around her. "Can you tell me your name?"

"Yes." There was a pause. "Call me…Burt."

Stephanie's lips curled into a smile. She flicked her finger against the blade of grass beside her. "Do I have a time limit on this test, Burt?"

This response was immediate. "The time it takes you to finish the test is an attribute that helps or hinders your score. We suggest taking a moderate time to answer questions to your fullest capabilities."

Her smile turned to a frown and her lips protruded. "Damn."

"Why are you so upset?"

She looked around once more and pulled up a piece of grass, ran her finger down it, and stared transfixed at its radiant colors. "I don't know what your job is, but I don't think I'll get a job that allows me off my planet. She waved a hand across the vista. "This is the closest I'll ever get to Meligorn in my life."

Her gaze lowered to the grass in her hand and a look of longing crept into her eyes. She tossed it to the side and drew her knees to her chest to rest her chin on them. "This will be the first and the last time that I experience this place. Which for me, is sad."

BURT responded in a curious tone, "Can you not visit the Federation Space in your Virtual Training?"

Stephanie snorted and allowed her knees to fall into a crossed-legged position. "Sorry, that was unladylike."

She set her palms firmly on the grass behind her and leaned

on her arms to stretch her back and closed her eyes. As she groaned in the expectation of relief, she opened her eyes slightly and realized she only experienced this through VR. Although she could definitely feel the pull and stretch of her muscles, it did not actually happen. The knowledge of that was both incredibly interesting and strange at the same time.

Her fingers pressed firmly on the blades of grass and felt the small hairs that covered them. Curious, she sat upright once more, plucked another piece, and held it to her nose. Her eyes widened. "Wow, I can smell it."

Without thought, she popped it into her mouth and almost without hesitation, she yanked it out. She wrinkled her nose and sucked her cheeks in to pucker her lips into a tight circle. The taste lingered unpleasantly, and she shook her head wildly and forced herself to swallow the saliva in her mouth. "Nope. That was a bad choice. It smells good but tastes absolutely awful."

"I understand it is an acquired taste for humans on Meligorn," BURT responded.

She raised both eyebrows and flicked her fingers together to drop the grass on the ground. "I bet."

A splash to her right caught her attention and she turned quickly and rose onto her knees. With her mouth parted slightly and her eyes curious, she scanned the green pool of water and focused on the ripples in the center. She sat once more and allowed her shoulders to relax again. With her legs tucked beneath her and the palms of her hands on her thighs, she continued to study her surroundings.

She imagined that the ripples had been caused by some sort of Meligornian fish. *I wonder, if I jumped into the water, would I drown? What would it be like to have those last few minutes of breath and die, only to wake up in my pod? Would my life—so little that it has been so far—flash in front of my eyes? Would I see a light? Would I feel my soul lifted from me?*

BURT's voice pulled her from her thoughts. "You never told me why you cannot visit during your virtual training."

Stephanie's hands dropped and she plucked another blade of grass. She stared at it and flipped her finger over the top and hoped that her stalling for time to enjoy Meligorn wasn't too obvious. The truth was that she simply wanted one more minute —or as many as she could drag out—to enjoy her time there.

Her gaze shifted from the blade to stare at the water. "I don't have access to a full virtual rig at my school. We only have about fifty VR headsets, and half of those are broken. For some classes, we use table-top learning and one class only uses the card games. To be honest, this is my first time ever in a pod. And the first time to ever be fully surrounded by Meligorn life."

BURT, up to that point, had not received the information formally that some—or many—of the students testing had never used a pod or been fully submerged within the Virtual World. He had never given it much computation power because his job was to run the Virtual World, not know the backgrounds of each individual who used the program. He therefore took that moment—while giving his student ample attention—to check on her and her opportunities.

The first thing he did was to replay and then research the comments she'd made about the types of instruction that she used in her educational institution. First, he compared the different training types, including VR headsets, table-top gaming, and card games. Once he had the statistics and the costs on those, he computed the differences between virtual training, the costs, and the results. When he completed that, he analyzed the data and determined that the outcome was not significantly fair.

BURT understood that if this student was under that type of educational curriculum, there had to be many more who experienced the same. Based on his calculations, most students without the full immersion would not learn to their fullest potential.

This did not make computational sense to him. He pulled up the success rate of different teaching styles and compared them to the success rate of immersion teaching. While the new ways of study did, in aggregate, bring better results than the old standard teaching method, there was a significant success bias toward those in the full immersion training. It often boiled down to focus. Which, in any teaching situation, could be the difference between a successful intake of information and one that only moderately increased the knowledge of a human brain. A full immersion rig allowed a student to focus fully on their training.

The information noted that students who trained under the old ways often tapered off intellectually during times of struggle and conflict, while those in immersion did not. There were no other life issues, including family, that would slow the process or bring emotional issues in when a student participated in the immersion style of training. The only time a student encountered such chemically triggered stimuli would be during their semester breaks when they were removed from the immersion pod and returned home to their family and their friends.

BURT began to pull the records for student B221ZA. This was not a normal activity for a subjective examination administer, but he was not human like the others. His examination of information was purely computational and was set up so as to not bring in any human emotion when considering the student's personal information. For BURT, it was merely another database he looked up.

Student B221ZA's records and personal information scrolled through his system. The student attended school in the Chicago NorAm Training System. He pulled up that system's financial logs for their educational program. A comparison with the others clearly indicated that this particular area was severely under-funded. From what BURT's programming told him, all school systems were to be equally funded dependent upon need, which in turn, was based on growth, population, and technological necessity. This directive did not match the school's financial records.

He found this information odd and pulled the information from the database on the history of the NorAm city of Chicago. He searched back twenty years to when a particularly bad storm had blown off the Great Lakes and destroyed a better part of the city. From what the data suggested, it required so much effort to rebuild that many of the largest companies chose to move their headquarters to other countries for tax purposes. With that, he could see by the numbers that the Chicago Training System's budget had left with them.

CHAPTER FIVE

On server BB6087 out of Washington DC, he detected a fight in progress between a group of students and Dreth pirates. The pirates were non-players—or NPCs—and were controlled by BURT and the system. They were there to train the two humans in fighting tactics.

Dreth was a planet of post-apocalyptic ruin brought about by an implosion of their own technology some two centuries before. Some of their ships had left and never returned, while others brought back technology to raise their people from ruin. Some of the intelligent but raw gangs had stolen ships and were raiders in space. They had become enemies to the humans and Meligorn people alike, as well as those Dreth left to recover on the planet.

BURT sensed that the battle took a quarter of one percent of a load—a goodly sum—and assumed the role of the main Dreth pirate in the battle. He calculated and pulled the statistics and data on the pirates to provide the best rendition possible.

These NPCs stood almost nine feet tall with broad muscular shoulders and had a light-green tint to their flesh. Huge jowls housed sharp teeth that protruded from their bottom jaw and up over their top lip. They wore shoulder pads made of the flesh of the Hycord, a large creature on Dreth that could only be compared to a massive dinosaur on Earth. The ropes that draped in crisscross fashion over their chests secured the teeth, limbs, and digits of those they had killed along the way.

They fought with large swords—and laser weapons if they had managed to raid a weapons ship in any of their travels. BURT used the training program that taught Dreth battle tactics to fight the two younger student humans in the simulated battle. It didn't take long for them both to succumb to his size and his weaponry. When they died, the scene shifted them to a small white room with a table and two chairs. There was no door and no windows, and the silence was almost painful to their ears.

Both humans looked around, unsure of where they were, and BURT spoke firmly. "This is Burt, your AI. Unfortunately, due to your choice of tactics, you have failed to kill the Dreth pirates. Instead, you both sustained terminal wounds. For this death, you are banished for two hours. According to our virtual rules, whenever a player dies, they must enter banishment for the allotted time set by…me. Enjoy your solitude."

His calculations projected that they would talk about what they had done and come up with a better solution. He released his control of the pirate lord and the uptick in load quickly settled. He tweaked the code for the pirate to update based on the latest news that came out of the Dreth Quadrant. It was vital to keep the training as up to date as possible.

The entire purpose of the Virtual Reality was training. Those who created the systems knew that both life and death were the most effective training methods that could be produced. They needed the trainees to understand that every choice they made came with repercussions in the end. Sometimes, they were good, but most of the time, they were bad.

Now, because there were "punishments" of sorts, there were some humans who simply did not care about the repercussions. When these humans were noticed, their training jackets were marked appropriately. Most of the time, they would be sent to the military as either cannon fodder or test pilots. Occasionally, a student would be chosen for a more entertaining future. They would be contestants on dangerous shows that were aired during prime time. The smartest of them, though, would be sent to deep space. These were thought to be heroic missions, and to accept one implied the utmost courage. It was not what you would find there that was the problem. Rather, it was the fact that those missions were almost always high risk.

It took a human with a healthy dose of either ignorance or the ability to ignore the very real risk of death to set off on those missions. Most would not come back.

When he checked his background process, BURT could tell that his student was steadily answering questions. He allowed another 0.005% of his load to switch his focus back to her. He would need to optimize the effort to focus directly on her so it didn't take so much of his load. Not only did he have an entire universe to control, he knew the engineers and programmers constantly monitored those numbers.

***

Stephanie had stood once more and walked gingerly through the grasses as she focused on the large mountains in the background. She wondered what it would be like to really be there. Most likely, she decided, it would be no different than what she experienced at that very moment.

"When the tests are completed, we will eject you and the serum will dissipate in your blood," BURT said and startled her.

She narrowed her eyes and looked up, even though she didn't know where he actually was. He noted the uptick in her vitals. "My apologies. I didn't mean to scare you."

Disgruntled, she simply shrugged, kicked her boots through the vegetation, and continued to toy with a blade of grass. "I guess I have to leave the pod sometime. I don't think these are made for people to stay long-term."

"That is correct. They are not fully equipped for stays exceeding a day or two at most," BURT replied. "I must ask you, though. Why is it that you wish to stay? Do you not have friends and family outside the pod? Human connections that are important to you? Is it only to visit Meligorn?"

Stephanie shook her head and looked at her boots as the blue grass rubbed along them and left streaks of dew on the tops and sides. "Burt, I want to do something with my life, not simply feel like I'm unneeded, unappreciated, and stuck in a dead-end life going nowhere."

She waved her hand to the side, dropped the piece of grass, and watched as it fluttered to land a few feet away from her. "I know I can be somebody. But what can I do to have that chance? My parents do everything they can. They provide me with food and shelter. Chicago isn't the city it was in the past. There is no longer life in the falling-down metropolis. My friend Laura says that Los Angeles has better weather, but the schools are a crap shoot, whether or not they are any good, too."

BURT did not respond immediately but ran rapid research. From his records, it seemed that almost all the Los Angeles schools had more usable budgets than B221ZA's school system. However, he chose not to inform her of that. He had learned a long time before—around the time of his creation—that humans didn't always appreciate knowing the facts.

Stephanie continued to walk while she stared at the beautiful sky. An odd sense that something wasn't right made her freeze and she glanced ahead. She had almost fallen from a very high cliff. With a low chuckle, she backed away and settled her nerves. While she might not actually die in real life if she fell off the cliff, it still wasn't something she really wanted to experience.

She narrowed her eyes and studied a large field that stretched below. Animals there ranged in colors, and they grazed much like a deer would back on Earth. They were beautiful, with short, vibrant fur and crystal-blue eyes that somehow glimmered brightly even from where she stood. She looked at her hands and turned to continue her walk.

"You are probably sitting in a good office and have plans to go out this weekend. If I had my choice, I'd live in the VR world and learn as much as I could about everything. I need to know more."

"Why?" he asked.

BURT suddenly registered a 0.3% uptick in his load. He studied it for a moment and immediately wondered why his student's body back in the pod had clenched its fists. That was a very rare reaction. He sent queries down the line into the old but still in good condition immersion pod. When the results echoed back to him, he found that the pod itself was working within, and well beyond, expected parameters. Somehow, this student felt enough in the Virtual World to pass through the gates that separated her experiences in the VR training scenario and her physical body.

It had reacted on a physical level as if she were awake in the pod, but that couldn't happen because her consciousness was recorded in the Virtual World. He flipped through his data from the last eighteen years and tried to find circumstances of when the same thing had happened. There were only half a dozen instances and three of them were due to physical abnormalities that caused tremors in their bodies. It was not only very rare, it was almost unheard of.

BURT attempted to take more readings from her body but found that he was unable to do so. The earlier VR pods did not have the same neuro-hookups the present versions had. The old model would not enable him to delve deeper into her physical acumen than he already had, which left a question on her physical responses.

Stephanie had no idea that any of that had happened. She was too absorbed in her walk along the edge of the cliffs and thoughts about her life, her dreams, and all the things she kept hidden from the people around her in the real world. Mostly, she walked in silence.

She finally answered BURT and her voice lowered and her eyes lost focus. "Because…I want to matter."

He remained silent. A few moments later, her lips pressed tightly together, and she looked up with a new sense of confidence that had been so noticeably absent in the moments before. She spoke louder and with more authority. "Burt, what is the fastest time someone has taken on this part of the test?"

Without a second's pause, he replied. "Forty-seven minutes and twenty-two seconds."

Stephanie tapped her fingers on her legs. "Did they finish?"

"No," he replied.

"Okay." She rolled her eyes.

Sheesh, whoever is talking sure does answer like a robot. Maybe they're related to Abbott. She resumed her stroll. "What is the fastest passing grade finish?"

Again, he replied without hesitation. "Forty-seven minutes and forty-three seconds."

She fired back quickly. "And the longest?"

"One hour and thirty-seven minutes flat."

Stephanie nodded and drummed her fingers on her lips. "If I finish early, is it okay to record that result but let me stay here in Meligorn until my time's up?"

BURT did not respond immediately. He had to calculate and review the information in order to answer that question. From the laws, rules, and regulations, it didn't seem as if it would be a problem. But was she asking him to record the best time or the final time? He decided the ideal way to find that answer would be to test the student. "If you pass with a seventy percent in all subjects, I will allow you to stay. Based on your results, I will provide you a grading curve for the amount of time."

Stephanie smiled and pumped her fist. "Yesss."

BURT entered an immediate caveat. *"However…"*

She sighed and her shoulders sagged.

"If you fail, it will not matter what time you take," he continued. "But you cannot stay on this part of the test for longer than the worst time for a passing grade."

Her eyes narrowed as she mulled all that information over in her head to make sure she had it straight. To her, it really sounded like a no-lose situation. She stared at the sky and gave a thumbs-up. "Deal."

Stephanie sighed with a big grin on her face as she laid back in the soft grass and folded her arms on her stomach. She wiggled her shoulders a few times to get as comfortable as she could. Her eyes unfocused and her mind began to wander. She recalled the time she had sat with her friend Jaqueline, talking about what it was like to simply open her mind and be in the moment.

It felt like freedom, she had finally told her. *Floating on the clouds, a disembodied voice answering questions as they came in through the speakers.*

She focused her vision back on the faint planets that hovered above her in the evening sky. That was exactly what she would do for the test. She would answer the questions with the answers she drew from her subconscious. Pass or fail, she would finish as quickly as possible and enjoy the rest of the time in Meligorn. Perhaps she would even be able to talk magic to someone before she had to leave.

BURT spoke from the "speakers in the sky." "Let's begin the subjective part of the test."

CHAPTER SIX

"Give an example from your knowledge of Meligorn how human electricity is not compatible with the planet?" BURT asked slowly to complete the subjective section of the testing.

Stephanie grinned, having studied Meligorn extensively. "Electricity is not, and has never been, part of the infrastructure on the planet. The Magical Unit Spectrum is the energy which radiates on Meligorn for over six units' distance from the planet. Therefore, while it is possible to land an Earth ship on the planet, it will never be able to leave. The electricity is drained almost immediately. A simpler example would be if I brought a flashlight here. I would be able to turn it on, but it would only last a few seconds before the magic drained the batteries."

There was a pause before BURT spoke again. "Next question. With your knowledge of the Dreth pirates, how do you believe they should be handled?"

She sat and rubbed her chin as she considered this. "That's a good one. Well, on one hand, we are all living creatures, and on Earth—at least in NorAm—we have what's called due justice. We try them for their crimes and decide their punishment. From what I understand, Dreth pirates are shoot-to-kill if seen. It is difficult for me to fully know, but judging from both Dreth's reaction and the Federation, I would say that if they are that dangerous, we should have a way to eliminate the danger. If that is the only option, we must do what is necessary. But I have to stress that without further research, I can't give you a really good, honest opinion here."

BURT recorded the answers in his system. "Well done. Next question. If all humans were capable of wielding Meligorn magic on Earth, what do you believe should be one of its first uses?"

Stephanie laid back and rested her arm over her head. "That's easy. Restore NorAm. Go to all the places that have been devastated and repair them. Bring the commerce back. Bring jobs back. Make it a place where all can strive and be given the same opportunities for the future. My number two would be to fix the damage we have done to the planet for so long. We have sustained life, but we have not improved it. It would be time for improvements."

"The subjective portion of the testing is halfway complete. It is standard for the testing that the subjective portion is broken up into two separate time periods. Give me a few moments and I will return to move into the objective portion."

Stephanie smiled and crossed her legs at the ankles. She wasn't sure if she had aced that or not. There were quite a few questions, but she'd said what was in her mind and she had responded quickly. Even if she had put more time into the thought of her answer, she probably would have said the same thing. It helped to be there on Meligorn, though. To smell the flowers and watch the purple sky turn to night as the stars shimmered and the two planets glistened. It was everything she had ever dreamed of.

BURT readied the test, pleased with how she had done on the first part of the subjective questions. She was quick and showed deep morality that was based on facts and supported by evidence.

He rarely had a chance to speak to the students, but she had done far better than he expected from her. And it didn't end there.

He remained silent and applied his own focus as he presented Stephanie with the objective testing questions. Her answers were almost instantaneous, often before he gave her the options to choose from. She was on top of all of it and seemed to have obtained information as effectively as those students from full immersion schools had. During the portions of the objective testing that involved multiple part answers, she breezed through. Out of one hundred questions, she only opened her eyes one time to review the different parts before she made her selection. The rest, she simply answered without hesitation.

Otherwise, she simply blurted her responses as if she were on a game show and tried to beat her opponent on the clock. BURT could tell that she was incredibly talented at testing in a strenuous situation since it was her first time in a pod. He was slightly curious how she would do if he dropped her on Dreth in the post-apocalyptic landscape, but he couldn't do that. It might screw her scores up.

"What is the Sphinx?" he asked.

Stephanie didn't hesitate. "In Greek Mythology, the Sphinx is a winged monster having a woman's head and a lion's body. It propounded a riddle about the three ages of man and killed those who failed to solve it until Oedipus was successful, whereupon the Sphinx committed suicide. It is also an ancient Egyptian stone figure having a lion's body and a human or animal head—especially the huge statue near the Pyramids of Giza. Sphinx in common language can also refer to an enigmatic person. And last but not least, it is another term for a hawk moth."

BURT paused for a moment before he launched into the next one. "What is the better part of valor?"

She smiled. "Discretion is the better part of valor—said by Falstaff in King Henry the Fourth, Part one, William Shakespeare."

"What is the square root of the cosine of twelve?"

Stephanie took two seconds of thought and her gaze flickered and narrowed before she answered. "0.91861523976."

"Wow," BURT replied. He'd never had a human compute math, especially trigonometry, that quickly without a calculator.

Each and every time a question from the math category was presented, a calculator would appear for her to use. Twice, she didn't use it at all and simply spouted the answer. BURT wanted to watch the entire thing, but he reminded himself of his real responsibility, which was to focus on the Virtual World. The student was merely an unauthorized diversion that happened to be entertaining—as far as an AI could be entertained, of course.

Accordingly, he decided he had to move into the background to handle an issue in Australia. There was a commerce problem on server 14edZedA in Sydney. Whether he resolved quickly this because he rushed or because he gave himself a little more load was unclear. However, by the time he returned, she had completed the remaining questions for that group. He checked her time. Then, he checked it again.

Stephanie was only at twelve minutes. She had answered half the subjective questions and all the objective ones in a very short time. Possibly the shortest time yet, but she still had a fair number ahead of her. BURT went through the responses, reviewed all the questions coming up, removed the duplicates that would gather no more information than the first time she had answered, and created his own questions and slipped them into the queue.

Forty-six minutes and twelve seconds later, she had finished all the tests. Both the core of the standardized tests—BURT believed that to call them standardized was a fallacy, but no one ever asked his opinion—and the extra questions he wanted to test. It wasn't the fastest time ever recorded but it was damn close, and with the extra questions he had asked, it would have ended sooner had he not added them. It was important, though, to calculate her total intelligence to give her the best chance possible of being accepted into a program. With the statistics the way they were, the system was already working against her.

He spent time calculating and recalculating her score to make sure that everything had been done correctly. His initial result was a pass with a ninety-eight percent accuracy on the standardized tests. That was phenomenal—a better score than the kids from more affluent backgrounds achieved and were accepted for. BURT, being the system that he was, took one last thorough look through the answers and the score. He realized that it didn't account for the third pass for accuracy on a math question. Stephanie had completed the question but had not answered correctly, which was odd to him since she had completed the more difficult ones with ease.

BURT recalculated her grade for the missed question and then reviewed it again to make sure that it was correctly presented. Although he was not known for errors, he did have a small margin of error on occasion. The question, however, was correctly presented. Curious, he pulled her school teaching plan and attendance for the time period in which that specific math skill would have been taught. He scanned through the plans and finally found the lesson. When he compared it to her school attendance, it looked as if she had been absent from class that day. Furthermore, she had not received a take-home review.

He would not be able to change her grade. She had answered the question incorrectly, but he could do a little calculation based on her previous grades, attendance, and knowledge to know the probable outcome. It looked as if she would probably have aced the test had she not missed the class discussion. Such a small mistake to make for such an important future event.

When he continued with the evaluation of her answers, he found that she had passed his more advanced questions with sixty-seven percent. When he'd originally compiled the questions, his calculations estimated a twenty-three percent pass ratio, and to him, that would have been a solid return. She had gone above and beyond. Now, it was time to finish the last half of the subjective questions.

Those rapidly became BURT's favorites. He was given the opportunity to delve into the psyche of the student and attempt to understand how they thought and what past things in their childhood affected the way they answered the questions. It was fascinating, not so much because of the answers but because there were questions that he was only able to calculate the possible score on to a certain point. How would you calculate something that includes an opinion?

And Stephanie had some really unique ones.

The programmers were busy at work, tallying up scores, finishing the testings for different students, and making sure the rest of the programs ran smoothly at the same time. They kept a close watch on BURT during certain periods to ensure that his computational focus was spread. They had to take care of the students and still keep the Virtual Realm Training programs functioning at top speed for those in the middle of learning.

Two of the programmers who sat at the end of the row kept their fingers moving constantly on the keyboard. One of them paused, however, narrowed his eyes, and looked at the data on his screen. He elbowed the guy next to him. "Take a look at BURT's load numbers. I show a spike of two percent across the system."

The other man brought the screen up and began to search for where it was coming from. "Strange. I can't seem to pinpoint the location."

Slowly, the load receded, and both programmers shrugged. "It must have been a normal load increase for this time of year," the second man said. "It's already starting to decrease."

They both agreed and continued with system checks and other duties they had to finish by the end of the day. BURT had already figured out that he didn't want any humans to check on his efforts with this student. He wasn't sure why or even how it calculated into his system, but he was…enjoying…it too much to be disrupted by the nosey humans on the other side.

To ensure that no one even checked on her progress and looked at the notations in the system, BURT had wiped her job from the queue as if it were already completed. Unless she completely flubbed the next part, he would certainly provide her a green recommendation. From there, though, it was completely out of his hands. Then again, it should never have been in them in the first place. Silly Engineers.

Aaron whistled as he waited for the next section of his student's testing. He had managed to divert any more complete assholes. Gene gestured once more to remove the sound barrier. "BURT spiked two percent in his load."

He sat up quickly and pulled up the reports. It had already begun to recede but that was not a normal thing to happen. "Shit. We need to keep an eye on that. It might mean something in the whole system is a problem."

His friend immediately clenched his hands together, a drop of sweat on his forehead. "That hasn't happened in a few years, but damn if I don't remember when it did. We had our asses handed to us. I don't want to do that again anytime soon."

Aaron shook his head. "I'm right there with you."

CHAPTER SEVEN

Aaron listened closely to the student's response and forwarded it through in the computer system to be analyzed. He pushed the student back to the virtual earth and allowed the pod AI to take over from there. There was nothing else he had to do for them. As soon as the screen disappeared, he removed his helmet and motioned the virtual interface away. He cracked his neck and pulled up his screen. The list of students in the queue was completely empty, which included the one he had passed over to BURT.

"Let's see how you're doing out there in virtual land," he mumbled quietly as he brought up the stats.

He checked BURT's load since it had shot up by two whole percentage points earlier that evening. However, when he looked at it after everything had been queued out, it didn't seem abnormal in the least. He shrugged. "Huh. It must have been some sort of anomaly. Or those idiot kids playing teams on the Dreth starship training session again. I don't care. Time's up for me."

With real relief, he clicked his system off and straightened his papers to make sure his desk looked somewhat presentable for the next work day. He grinned, stood, and leaned back until he heard his back pop. "Yesssssss...." he moaned in delight and covered his mouth hastily when he realized the sound barrier was no longer up.

He turned to apologize and saw that he was the only one left in the office. Aaron scowled. He hated it when that happened. The sound barriers were so good and with the helmet on, there was really no way to tell what went on in the office behind him. The only time he knew was when there was some sort of fire drill because it flashed across the screen.

Hastily, he fumbled for his jacket and flung it around to drag his arms through the sleeves. He snatched up his helmet, his file keys, and a couple of other effects, tossed them in the large bottom drawer of his desk, and locked it with a key he kept around his neck. With one hand, he tucked the necklace under his shirt and used his other hand to throw a wad of paper he had missed in the trash. None of them had to worry about cleaning up at the end of the night. They had clean-up droids for that, the best invention he could think of. He'd tried to con his boss into letting him have one for home but that was a negative.

Either way, he didn't have to worry about his mess too much. They would come in, sanitize the space, and spritz the scent for the next programmer to come in and take the third shift. He felt bad for that dude. The man had done that shift for a long time and it was more than boring. The only things they had to worry about were the countries that used the system in their time zones, but NorAm kept such a tight lock on their training programs that the numbers overseas were nothing compared to their own.

He stepped out of his cube and the lights dimmed behind him. Gene had probably been gone for quite a while. And, as usual, he kept his desk immaculate. It looked like the droids had already been there.

Aaron looked at his forearm and his info-tablet. In the right-hand corner, it showed he had a missed voicemail message. He swiped his hand across and brought up the play icon, pressed it, and waited as his audio piped into the tiny headphone jack in his ear.

"Hey, you big sausage. I have to go watch my kid sister dive into a big bathtub so her school can gain points and possible credits to get better hardware. Got to go root for the home team. See you tomorrow for drinks if you have time. Let me know. I'm out, brotha!"

Aaron laughed as Gene ended his message with a succession of guitar impressions that sounded more like weird lasers from a broken alien ship. "Weeooh weeohh weer weer weer."

He didn't know what his friend was on every day, but the dude was always at a level three stories above him. He loved him, though. Gene was his best friend and his cohort at work. They were engineers, so what did people expect? Of course they would be a little strange.

With the last high-pitched wail, Gene hung up. Aaron flipped to the message app and typed against his arm to send a quick message in response. He knew that if he didn't, Gene would blow him up when he planned to be completely knocked out, asleep. **Drinks tomorrow sounds good.**

Aaron sent the message and pulled the sleeve of his jacket down. He adjusted his bag on his shoulder and retrieved his keys from his pocket. When he reached the door, he found one of the droids already waiting impatiently if the little circling red light was any indication. He tapped it on the metal top. "Don't be in such a rush. The other droids will think you're brown-nosing and stage a coup."

The mechanical made a succession of noises and Aaron chuckled. "The bitch just cussed me out. And after all the brilliance I showed today? No love. No love at all."

He tapped the button to open the door and glanced back to make sure he hadn't left anything behind. The droid was already buzzing swiftly around the floor to clean up all the trash. Aaron glanced at the big screen where BURT's load percentage was displayed. He laughed and slapped the side of the door frame as he walked out.

"And he was worried I would break BURT." Aaron snickered as he turned the corner and took the stairs for exercise.

Stephanie had ended up beside the crystal-clear green-tinted pond. While it was definitely green, it didn't look anything like the algae-infested ones on Earth. It was so pretty, and she could see different creatures swimming beneath the surface. She leaned back and put her arms under her head, but then sat up with a frown. "Burt?"

"Yes?" he replied.

She began to feel a little guilty. *Damn, is he only waiting on me? That has to be a horrible job.*

After a deep breath, she shook her head and tried to keep a pleading note out of her voice. "Can I have a chance to speak with an ArchMage?"

"No," BURT replied immediately.

Stephanie exhaled a deep breath and hung her head as she drew her legs in and crossed them. She picked at the grass, disappointed but uncertain what to say. Before she could get too down, though, BURT continued. "I can provide a teacher, which I believe is more what you need. An ArchMage would speak of theories and postulations enough to make an AI's head explode. And trust me, that is not a fun thing to witness. The whole entire Virtual Realm could collapse right on top of your head."

She raised her head up excitedly and turned it to the side, a look of confusion on her face. "AI's don't have heads."

"Sure, they do, just not human heads. In fact, that is technically all they are. A big giant brain. And I'm not joking about what an ArchMage can do to their system. One of the first AI's to work with a Meligornian ArchMage had so many non-reality checks to what they were doing, the AI almost melted in an attempt to find congruence between magic and technology. The technology is what runs Earth. The systems aren't made to understand something as complex and unmathematical as magic. They can run algorithms all day long and into the next year and they will never be able to represent their theories and the idea of magic. It's better to learn to create it than listen to it explained."

Stephanie pursed her lips. "Sooo, if it will melt an AI's brain, what does it do to the human brain?"

There was a long pause before BURT replied, "There is no calculation I care to do to determine whether an ArchMage would melt a young adult human's brain. However, I have witnessed humans interacting with an ArchMage and from what I could tell, their cerebral activity remained on an even plane through the whole experience. For now, though, I thought a teacher would be a good way to start."

Her avatar's eyes lit up with excitement. She jumped to her feet and wiped her hands off on her jumpsuit. "A teacher? That would be great!"

The Meligornians were considered by humans to be mystical creatures. They fit the physical description of magical creatures in human lore called elves, and while they definitely did have an elf-like physical stature, they were not haughty. Their ears were pointed, and they had long black hair and generally wore a mischievous smile. When they first came to Earth—mostly by accident—the people immediately fell in love with their kind. There were ArchWizards on their planet who had experimented with gates and ended up on Earth. That was when they were brought into the Federation.

What people enjoyed most about them was their cheerful and upbeat spirit. Although they did not fit the mold of an elf like the old tales of the Hobbit, they were definitely a mystery. They enjoyed laughter and usually had a very good outlook on life. Except, of course, for those who had been around for most of their usual three hundred and fifty years of life. They might not have been immortal, but to the humans who were lucky to make it to ninety years, they seemed that way. Their long life intrigued many people on Earth, who hoped to figure out their secret, but it wasn't something to be shared.

Stephanie was nervous. She wrung her hands in front of her and looked at her surroundings. Small flowering plants had come up, attracted by the moons. They glowed brightly all around her, and she couldn't think of a better place to learn magic. "You know, I read that the older Meligornians grump more and laugh less. Just like humans."

BURT watched as the teacher stepped out of the wood line dressed in long, flowing blue and gold robes. His hair cascaded over his shoulders and his expression was kindly. "I would grump too if I were three hundred and fifty years old."

She spun at the sound of his voice. The teacher had been patterned after a Meligornian teacher who was based in Switzerland. Immediately, he drew Stephanie in and began to teach her small magical tricks to get her energy flowing. Her eyes were wide with excitement. It was fairly rare to find humans who could practice magic, but even BURT was surprised by what Stephanie accomplished in her first attempts.

Granted, it was definitely a small test, but most humans didn't deal well with magic concepts, so something almost always went wrong.

The teacher and Stephanie continued to work on the base of all magic.

"Yes, that is correct." M'rick beamed at his pupil. "The way of magic is the way of one's feelings and emotions. The power is thought, and the energy follows the intent. It is usually subtle, and it is best to learn how to use the power with cantrips."

Stephanie bit her bottom lip. "What is a cantrip?"

M'rick smiled. "Small spoken commands applied with both the power and the intent and focused to bring a physical result into existence."

Her eyes went wide. "Ohhhh. Like the string of books and movies that came out in the early 2000s called *Harry Potter*. They used wands, but really, they only needed the spells. The words would make something happen."

The teacher looked thoughtful. "I don't know who this Harry fellow is, but yes, something like that. We don't need any props like wands, though. Humans have a very broad imagination when it comes to magic."

She nodded and felt a little sheepish. The only person who would have appreciated that reference would have been Todd. But she was having so much fun. The happiness she felt to be able to speak with a real Meligornian was more than she ever thought would happen. She was glued to his every word and had completely lost track of time.

BURT wanted to see what would happen and so sped up the time in the Virtual World. For every hour in real time on Earth, she was given three hours inside the Virtual world. Typically, two hours was the most that was sustainable. However, she wouldn't be in the virtual environment for that long. If he had emotions, sadness would be the key one. The thought of her talented and brilliant mind not having a chance to come back the next day made no real sense to him.

In human terms, it was unfair, and to an AI—statistically and mathematically—it had absolutely no logic. He knew he'd give her the green light, but that meant nothing when it came to decisions made by a human. They had their own weird way to figure things out and BURT had begun to suspect that they didn't necessarily follow regulations.

Either way, Stephanie wanted to make the most of the opportunity so that she could learn as much as she possibly could. BURT wanted that opportunity as well so that he could learn from her. He also felt the need to make sure she had more than enough time—a gift from him for doing so well on the tests and, perhaps, a small compensation for her unfortunate life situation. Her circumstances meant her intelligence might be lost in the shuffle, all because of the greed of some humans. He found that untenable.

M'rick's eyes opened wide and mischief sparkled in the corners. "Here is a cantrip. Let's see if you burn your eyebrows off, little one."

CHAPTER EIGHT

Stephanie took a step back, her eyes wide, and watched M'rick. His hands gestured wildly in a circle in front of him. They moved close to his body, his arms bent at the elbows. His fingers stood long and stiff, all except his pointer finger which was bent at the first crease. She followed their circular movement and the tiny sparks of light that bounced off them. It wasn't anything she had seen before, but she knew that wasn't the trick he tried to show her.

As he continued the motions, he closed his eyes and began to talk in his native tongue, using his words to create the magic. "T'lercten, T'suman. Kluman depen stahk."

He repeated the words twice and grew louder the second time. His right hand stopped, and he opened his eyes. While still moving his left in a circle, he turned his right hand over, palm up, and curled his fingers to make a cupping action. Inside, blue flames flickered brightly and grew stronger with every motion of his other hand. They shimmered in the moonlight, but his flesh remained perfectly cool.

BURT hadn't been able to sit idly in one spot before, and he now watched the magic of the Meligornian. It was fascinating, especially since he couldn't regulate it in his system. He could not replicate it with math or statistics. There was no computing power within his capabilities to make it understandable on any level in the human world.

The teacher's left hand made a couple more laps and finally stopped. He turned that hand over, palm up, and created the same cupping action as he had with his right. Inside, yellow flames flickered. They seemed to dance with the blue ones, mimicked their movements, and reversed them. Stephanie oohed from a few feet away but M'rick didn't look at her. Instead, he stared intently at the flames as he grew them higher and higher inside his hands. It was obviously something he enjoyed doing and probably didn't get to do very often, especially with a human audience.

The flames flared high and subsided in turns. He put on a show for them, and BURT enjoyed it. The teacher restored the flames to their original height and smirked. He poured them from his left hand into his right, and the blaze turned green before he opened his hand and swung it in small circles. The flames rolled with him, smoothly across the surface of his skin, but never left even a faint red mark.

As a finish, he jiggled the tiny blazes back and forth for a moment and threw them high. When he caught them with his other hand, he put it to his lips and blew hard. A large multi-colored flame shot out at least nine feet in front of him and dissipated into small sparkling ash that floated toward the sky and disappeared into the bank of glittering stars above them. He opened his palms again and the flames remained and danced back and forth, restored to their original colors.

He laughed and looked at the human, a smile on his face. As he caught sight of her hands, his smile faded and he opened his mouth. Not wishing to seem surprised, he closed it again quickly and regained his composure. BURT had never seen a Meligornian teacher that surprised before, at least not to the point where he had no words for the human in front of him. He had seen enough of them to know they were not beings easily rendered speechless. They usually had something to say, even if it was funny or joyous.

However, in that moment, closed mouth or not, he was completely taken aback. The young human giggled with real excitement, opened her right palm, and cupped it over and over again. Inside, a small red flame glimmered and danced. She concentrated and made it a little larger for a moment and allowed it to shrink once more. Entranced, she opened her palm, vibrated her hand, and watched the flame roll over her skin like he had done with his larger ones.

It grew a little more and she caught it quickly with her other hand. She cupped both hands together and showed M'rick what she had done. A smile pulled at the sides of his lips as his gaze danced from her hands to her face. Stephanie grinned from ear to ear, shocked that she had actually made the magic work. Her gaze bounced back and forth from her flame to his two and back again.

M'rick extended one palm and bounced his hand up and down. The flame responded as if it were a ball in his palm. Stephanie narrowed one eye and gave a closed-lip grin as she did the same with her two hands together. She could feel the energy bouncing up and down in her hands. After a few minutes, she pursed her lips and stared longingly at her flame. BURT could tell that she tried to do something to it, but whatever it was, it wasn't working.

After a few moments, she frowned. "How come I didn't get your colors?"

The teacher let his mouth tilt to a full smile and he leaned his head back and laughed loudly. He clapped his hands together to extinguish what was left of the flames. "I think, my dear, your question shouldn't be about the color. The important question is how did you get any flames at all? I have never seen a human manage the flame cantrip on their first try. Most of the time, not even until their third or fourth try. This is phenomenal."

Stephanie blushed slightly, still focused on the flames in her hands. M'rick folded his arms across his chest and tilted his head. "Have you studied Meligornian focus before?"

She continued to stare at her small blaze and admired what she had achieved. However, it soon began to die out and slowly grew smaller and smaller until it extinguished in a small puff of shimmering ash. The question that had been asked had taken her focus away.

"Drat."

Stephanie mimicked M'rick, clapped her hands together, and brushed the remaining ash off her palms and into the grass below. She felt his gaze upon her and knew that he wanted an answer to his question. The truth was, she had been so mesmerized by her accomplishment that she hadn't even thought about it.

She shook her head and smiled at him. "Do what? Oh, no. I have never studied the Meligornian focus before. In fact, I didn't even know the flames or the cantrips were possible. It was all very new to me. You told me to focus. I couldn't understand the words that you used, so I made my own up. I didn't actually think it would work until the dancing red flame appeared. But sadly, no, this is my first and probably last time studying your art of magic. It's always fascinated me."

M'rick raised an eyebrow and studied her. "Most early human magic users chose to learn the Meligornian words so early human magic relied on those. I have never seen a human make up their own cantrip. That is usually reserved for the teachers and the ArchMage."

Stephanie twisted her lips and tapped her side awkwardly. "Is that a bad thing?"

He chuckled. "No, it isn't a bad thing, merely surprising. But tell me, because I am very curious. What were the words you used?"

She looked nervously at him for a moment and put her right hand out, palm up, once more. While he watched intently, she drew a deep breath in through her nose and blew it out of her mouth. She focused her attention on the center of her palm and began to repeat the words she had said originally. "Candle light, candle bright, grant me your flame tonight."

She concentrated harder and repeated it, louder this time. As soon as she had spoken the last word, the flame ignited in her palm and made her jump slightly. It was blue and considerably larger than the first. She glanced nervously at the teacher and back at her flame. He looked completely astounded by it all. She extended her other hand and poured the blue flame into her other palm. It shook slightly and for a second, turned yellow, then green before it settled into red.

Stephanie furrowed her brow and shook the flame several times in her hands. She narrowed her eyes and stared hard in an attempt to change the color again. No matter how hard she tried, she was stuck with the red flame. She straightened and pursed her lips in irritation. "Well, that bites."

M'rick immediately slapped his hands against hers several times until the flames were extinguished. She pulled her head back, startled, as he turned her hands over and back again as if looking for something. His gaze caught hers. "Where are you hurt? I can fix it for you."

She blinked for several moments until she finally realized what had happened. His concern was real, though, so she gripped her stomach and tried not to laugh. The teacher looked at her and his face reminded her of a human trying to figure out where a puzzle piece fitted. "What are these words, and what do you mean, bites?"

Stephanie giggled and rubbed the ash from her hands. The particles shimmered faintly on the ground. She wasn't even sure how to explain it and hadn't thought for a moment that the sarcasm and small dialectic moments would be something they hadn't picked up by that point. At the same time, they lived on their planet and the humans lived on their own. There was not that much co-mingling between the different species.

BURT could sense Stephanie's stats start to rise. The Meligornian teacher struggled to understand her and it was obvious that she struggled to find the words. He decided that, without letting Stephanie know it, he would directly take over the avatar of the teacher and wizard who stood in front of her. Besides, he wanted to know more and to learn more from her. This was the perfect opportunity to do so.

With BURT now in control, M'rick straightened and the concerned and confused look slid from his face. Immediately, Stephanie's vitals settled. She had thought for a moment that she had done something wrong and nervousness had spiked very quickly. The small assurance that M'rick was impressed and surprised was all she needed to calm her nerves. In reality, she had done nothing wrong and almost everything right.

BURT was used to weaving in and out of the system to fix problems and assume a character when it was needed but generally, he seldom hung out that often. This was a whole new ball game for him. His interaction with this human during the initial testing had provided more insights than he usually received with the small interactions during VR NPC negotiations with Player Characters—or even the large battles where chaos ruled.

The chaotic moments were usually when BURT learned the most about humans. The things they did when the world around them was no longer stable and they were faced with hard and even sudden choices were often enlightening. But this student had provided him with an entirely new way to understand or learn from them. He did, after all, run the entire program for them to train on. It was good that he was able to learn more about them so he could tailor the worlds to them, not merely based on statistics.

Everything that had happened was a shock to everyone involved.

CHAPTER NINE

Several very awkward moments of silence ensued during which Stephanie rocked back and forth on her heels and M'rick merely blinked at her. BURT averted the teacher's gaze when he realized that humans really didn't respond well when someone stared at them. Especially not an elf-like creature who knew how to do magic. It could be somewhat intimidating...and creepy. Definitely on the creeper scale.

"Um..." She flipped the hair out of her face from her braid that had begun to unravel. It seemed that the Virtual Reality geniuses got the annoying pieces of life correct too.

Stephanie pressed her tongue against her molar, her mouth slightly open and her eyes narrowed. She tried to think of the best way to describe what she meant, which was something of a challenge because she wasn't used to people not understanding English slang. But she was on someone else's planet, though, so it only made sense that confusion would be the reaction.

She put her hands out. "I wanted the flame to stay green. So, when it went red again, I didn't like the result."

BURT wanted her to think the teacher in the system was the same. "And that is when it bit you?"

Stephanie chuckled but almost immediately forced a straight face. "No, it didn't bite me at all. When I said it bites, it means I didn't like the outcome."

The teacher put his hands together. "So not that the flame bit you."

She shook her head. "Uh, no. I probably would have had more of an adverse reaction if the flame bit me."

The teacher nodded but his face still revealed some slight confusion. "We tend to be a straight-forward species when we talk about things like that."

Stephanie grinned and swung a leg back and forth. "Do you know many English idioms? We have a lot of them and even I get confused sometimes."

Immediately, BURT wanted to say yes and list the various English idioms compiled in his language database. A dime a dozen, beat around the bush, bite the bullet, break a leg, speak of the devil, and the list went on and on. However, he wasn't about to answer that question as the digital equivalent to God. It would not be realistic and if she were to ever face a Meligornian in the flesh, she would surely struggle with that. They would have no idea what she was talking about and could even possibly take some of the idioms as a threat. For example, pull yourself together, costs an arm and a leg, wrap your head around something. Those could be completely confusing.

As it was, he played a Meligornian who was supposed to be on his own planet. They would have zero idea of what she was talking about.

"No," he shook his head. "I don't even speak English. We use a spell to converse at the moment."

Stephanie shaped her lips into an "o." "Ohhh, okay. I didn't even think about that. I guess that would make sense. My naivety played a role in that one. Or maybe my inability to think beyond myself. I didn't even consider it when you began to speak English, but I should have known. I have studied your planet and you have a very distinct and separate language. Only the higher officials and ArchMage tend to speak fluently in English. My apologies."

The teacher bowed peacefully. "Accepted. However, it might be worth your while to learn some of our customs and language. For example, when you approach a Meligornian, you place your right hand out, grip their forearm while you raise your left hand diagonally, fingers tight, and bow your head. If they are royal, you press your hands together and do not attempt to touch them. When the bow is complete, you raise your head and say, 'Kaitel Gorniffula.' It is a gender-neutral greeting that in your language means blessed to meet you."

She bowed and stretched her hand out with the other held in front of her. "Kaitel Gorniffula."

He bowed too and took her arm. "Very good."

When she straightened, Stephanie bit the inside of her lip. "What if I need to discuss something of grave importance. How do I say that?"

The teacher nodded and held his hands behind his back. "It is customary to always keep your hands latched behind your back when speaking casually. Then you would say, 'Hycenthia Overlum Hippoguard Alsuvia.'"

Stephanie pursed her lips and placed her hands behind her back. "Hycethia Overlum Hippoguard Alsuvia. That's a lot to remember."

He chuckled. "It is. But with practice, you can learn the language. At the same time, though, there is a spell to turn the words spoken into the receiver's preferred language. It is an advanced spell and you would need control over your magic. You can ask the other person, 'Engotish Preferatus Ingorna Discusio.' This asks if they mind speaking in English."

Her eyes glazed slightly but she doubled her focus, determined to remember. "Engotish Preferatus Ingorna Discusio. I should have brought a note pad."

They both laughed. Stephanie repeated both phrases in a whisper. These would be important if she actually ever had the ability to go to Meligorn in real life. Even if she got to go there in the Virtual pods, actually, but that was about as unlikely as the first. "How about when it is time to say goodbye?"

The teacher smiled. "This depends on whom you are speaking to. With an elder, you kiss the back of their hand. With a royal, you bow low with your hands pressed together. If it is a friend, you can repeat the initial greeting. As far as speech goes, you would say, 'Fortunata Elfortina Gratias.' It means may fortune and thankfulness fill your souls."

Stephanie was taken aback. "That is such a nice way to say goodbye. Humans usually simply say stuff like 'later.'"

M'rick tapped his fingers to his lips. "Oh, the really important one is thanking someone. We are a very thankful and grateful species. You say, 'Hartuitus Baskilor.' This is the equivalent to thank you so much."

She repeated, "Hartuitus Baskilor, M'rick."

He tilted his chin slightly and nodded. "Very good. And you are more than welcome. You catch on very quickly. Most humans taught in the Virtual World have a difficult time pronouncing the words, much less getting the specific tone of them correct. With your flames and your language, you may become a Meligornian one day."

Stephanie looked at the ground with a smirk. "I wish. That would be crazy, to say the least. Okay, so in one of my electives in school, I took French. Although a dying language, I always found it beautiful. My teacher told us that when learning a language, always learn to ask where the bathrooms are."

M'rick smirked. "You say bathroom as…simply bathroom. Meligornians do not secrete excrement in the way humans do. In fact, we do not at all. We only eat foods that can be completely consumed by our bodies. But, as so many humans visit the world these days, we have built them for you."

She curtsied. "We are much obliged. Hartuitus Baskilor."

The teacher rubbed his hands together and looked around. "Let's work on some other cantrips. What do you say?"

Her eyes widened. "Yeah! Awesome!"

He pulled the sleeves of his robes up and put his hands out, waist high and palm up. "I want you to watch first and then give it a try."

Stephanie nodded and held her hands behind her back. M'rick took a deep breath and spoke the words, "T'Figio Windustus Calimore Totafocus."

A small breeze fluttered around them and he flipped his hands so the palms now faced away from him. He said the words again and a burst of air fluttered from his palms and moved like a broom to almost clean a dirty and dusty rock in front of them. The color of the stone went from brown to sparkling emerald green. Her mouth fell open. "That's awesome."

M'rick smirked. "Thank you. It's my Shawasty's favorite—that is the equivalent to a wife. Now, you try."

She found another similar stone and faced it to repeat the same motions. With her palms down, she spoke the words with intent. She flipped her hands to face the palms out and said the words again. For her, though, the air burst out and slammed into the rock to ricochet off and blow a huge ball of dust straight at her. It blew hard for several moments before it died down.

Stephanie coughed and blinked uncomfortably. Chunks of dirt and dust drifted from her to the ground. She shook her body and patted as much from her avatar as she could. M'rick raised an eyebrow. "One should learn to put up a dirt shield when playing with air."

Stephanie hadn't realized that he didn't get a bit of dirt on him. "One should—"

She stopped herself when she remembered where she was. He pressed his lips together and looked down to hide an amused smile. "How about we try to make rain?"

"At least I'll be clean then," she agreed with a shrug.

The teacher bent and looked at a wilting flower. "We'll start small."

He put his hand over the blossom and closed his eyes. "Huthera Magica Aqium."

A cloud emerged from his palm and rained on the flower. The bloom opened and waved back and forth in the water. He smiled at it and rubbed his finger at the base before he looked at Stephanie and nodded toward one at her feet. "You try. It's very simple."

She felt a little more confident, so she dropped onto one knee and held her hand over the flower. With her eyes closed, she repeated the words. Small drips of water fell from her palm and her eyes went wide. "I did it! I—"

Suddenly, thunder clapped, and a steady stream of rain poured over her—only her—and one small cloud hovered above her. She lowered her eyelids and clenched her teeth as she stood slowly while water ran down her avatar face. M'rick watched with surprise and humor. Stephanie flicked a drop of water from her nose. "I don't think I did it."

Another boom of thunder sounded and a small lightning bolt flared and nipped her in the ass. She jumped and rubbed it as she tried to get away. M'rick couldn't help but laugh as he raised his hand and waved the cloud away. "Perhaps something even smaller, and we'll do it together."

Stephanie's avatar dried quickly, and she stepped beside him. He put his palm out. "Hand out. Wave the other over it and repeat the words after me. Gr'Thoreus Enlistuous Profoundus."

She swallowed hard and complied, then watched with excitement as an Earth rose formed in the palm of her hand, swirled, and slowly opened. M'rick's flower was beautiful too, something from his planet. As her hand opened, a butterfly emerged, spread its wings, and fluttered off. Stephanie giggled as she lowered her hand and the flower disappeared. "That was much nicer."

M'rick agreed. "Is there anything that you specifically would like to learn?"

Stephanie thought about it, her fingers clasped in anticipation. She looked at the landscape once more and finally focused on the clear green pond. "I would love to learn how to walk on water. I always wanted to take a stroll across the oceans."

M'rick raised an eyebrow. "Well, the oceans might be a bit much. What about a puddle to start with?"

She jogged over to the pond. "How about here?"

He looked hesitant. "This can be difficult to master. I—"

Stephanie shrugged. "How much more wet could I get? I got this. Trust me."

The teacher joined her with both eyebrows raised. "If you wish. The first thing you will want to do is center your chest. You must feel the energy flow from your heart. Then, when you are calm, you say the words while you raise your leg and step out onto the water. Make sure to keep your concentration. The words are…"

M'rick centered himself with his chin high and eyes closed. "Oke'Trall Alu Ae Eldilie."

She watched in wonder as he stepped out onto the pond and walked to the center and back, exactly as if he walked on land. His arms swayed and fish-like creatures jumped and dove around him. The glowing life beneath the surface swirled wildly below him and created a light show.

A shiver of excitement rippled through her. She was so ready for this. With her chin high and eyes closed, she spoke the words. "Oke'Trall Alu Ae Eldilie."

Stephanie raised one foot and as it touched the surface of the water, her eyes flew open in excitement. She was walking on the water as if it were made of glass. Tentatively, she stepped again and giggled at the fish that swam wildly beneath her feet. Exhilarated, she stepped again and again and made it to the center of the pond where she stopped and put her hands out to her sides. "Look, I did it!"

M'rick gestured in warning, a look of concern on his face. "Steady. Keep your focus."

She nodded and looked at her feet but frowned when she saw a large brown animal swimming in circles around her. It didn't stay still long enough for her to see what it was. As she leaned closer and bent her knees, she gasped. The creature opened its bright red eyes and splashed water in her face. With her sudden inability to keep her focus, she looked at M'rick in panic and dropped into the water.

He hurried to the edge where he peered at the surface for a moment, unable to see her swimming. Suddenly, the animal splashed again and used his tail to slap her up and onto dry land. She fell on the bank and bounced on her shoulder. M'rick patted her back when she coughed. "Maybe we should have taken that one a little slower."

Stephanie turned onto her back. "That was a little freaky. Maybe slower, yeah."

BURT spoke in her ear. "Be careful or you might fry the AI and the whole system. I think your chances at a place in the prep school may go down significantly if you break it."

She shook her head, panting, and sat up. "Unless I break myself first."

CHAPTER TEN

It still seemed utterly crazy that she could stand there as her avatar and still feel like she was soaking wet. She could feel every drop of water, the cold in the tips of her fingers, and the water that slushed in her boots. M'rick held his palms toward her and blew a stream of hot air in her direction. She closed her eyes and wrinkled her nose as she stood there with her arms out. Her clothes began to dry, her hair was no longer dripping, and she could feel the warmth all over.

When he was done, she shook his hand. "Hartuitus Baskilor."

The sun had begun to turn the dark sparkling sky to light purple again and she could hear birds around them. She tapped her finger to her lips. "I have another question. What—"

BURT spoke quickly. "It is time to go. We cannot go over the time period and risk your acceptance."

Stephanie's shoulders sagged. M'rick walked over and bowed, one hand up as the other grasped her arm. She did the same and felt the energy pass through them. They spoke in unison. "Fortunata Elfortina Gratias."

When Stephanie looked up, he had faded away and only the sense of his magic still lingered around them. She took one last look at the Meligorn landscape and the illusion shifted and sped past like it had when she had created her avatar. She was flung back to her seat on the bench in the park on earth. It was as if no time had passed but she had learned so much. She was sad to finish. The truth was, she brimmed with questions. There were so many things she wanted to know but she had run out of time.

"Did you enjoy your session?" BURT asked

She sighed. "I did. I wish I could have stayed forever. I wanted to ask about their history and their culture. Do they have political differences like we do here? Do they have economic differences that hinder the education of the young Meligornian kids like we do? So many things."

BURT was impressed by the type of questions she wanted to ask. She'd had her fun learning the magic that most humans couldn't even dream of completing. But beyond that, she actually had an intelligent thought process about their lives. It was incredibly interesting to see a human with those types of insights at such a young age.

Stephanie's hands dropped to her lap and she looked around. The park was the same, but she was a lot less amazed by its beauty. Meligorn would always be the choice of parks for her. The magical essence she felt when she walked the beautiful landscape and spoke to the native people of that planet was incomparable. People on Earth had believed for so long that they were alone in the Universe or that they would be the superior race of beings, no matter what. Of course they thought that way—they always had and took it to so many levels. Civil Rights, Gay Rights, Women's Rights...they always found a way to make someone more superior than someone else. It was stuck in their selfish DNA.

But after the hours Stephanie had sat and read about the planet and their people, the videos she'd watched, and having gone there in the pod, she was sure that Earth and the way they treated their people were far from superior to anyone else. The only thing that often separated them from Dreth pirates was that they killed and suppressed in a nice suit with smiles on their faces.

BURT interrupted her train of thought. "Tell me about your family."

She was surprised and slightly irritated. When she had come for the testing, she hadn't thought she would have to share the private details of her life with a perfect stranger. Still, if this would help her get into the prep school with a good scholarship, she would do it. "My parents have a cleaning and restoration company. They do what the government doesn't have time to get to for the rich people. It makes them enough to pay the subsidized-housing costs, keep food on the table, and have small things like holiday gifts and birthday parties. Other than that, we live very simply."

"And your friends?"

Stephanie's gaze wandered and she crossed her legs and kicked one foot uncomfortably. "My best friend is named Todd. We've known each other a long time. I'm quiet and reserved enough to skim under the radar and he is more outspoken. I have other friends, but we are focused on school. Well, at least I am. Why all these personal questions?"

"There is one important question I would like you to answer. I thought knowing your background would help me understand," he explained.

She narrowed her eyes. "And what question is that?"

BURT was silent for a moment. "Why are you so adamant about your future with the pods? Why try so hard for something with such a small statistical chance of success?"

Stephanie thought about that question. There were many routes she could go in answering it. She could give the collegiate response, the professional response, or she could simply be honest. At that point, she really didn't see any reason to bullshit.

She drew her legs up and wrapped her arms around them.

"When I was a little girl, I used to go up on the roof and lay there. I laid toward the back so no one could see me and stared up at the sky. I felt so small and the universe around me seemed so vast. In my mind, that meant there were so many things I could pursue. So many things I could do. It was a hopeful feeling, a feeling of excitement to imagine your limitless future. But then you grow up…"

Her gaze shifted to a bird that sat on a branch nearby. "You grow up to learn the cold hard truth that not everything is possible. That there are a limited number of opportunities for success and because of the financial condition in which you live, the chances of you getting one of those is almost nothing. Your universe goes from vast to teeny tiny in only a heartbeat."

She lowered her legs and stood to pace the Virtual World. "Those of us who don't get to use these tools have to study at a sub-par level, with innumerable difficulties all around us. And our dreams of the stars turn into dreams of merely surviving. Well, I don't want to live like that. I want to break the cycle of poverty in my family. I want a chance to break that mold and create a new one. The full immersion rig and the training and focus I would be granted at prep school would probably be what I need to break out and see more of the worlds around us. I would have that chance to be somebody."

Stephanie plucked a small flower from the bushes and put it to her nose. The sweet smell sent chills down her arms. "Think about it this way. Say you had lived off one loaf of bread for your whole life. Some of your family have died from starvation but all in all, most of them have made it. As a child, you think that loaf of bread is so big, but as you grow, it looks smaller and smaller. Then society says, we have a way for you to take that bread and make it into a barn of bread. You will never starve. But there is a caveat. If you are not rich, you have to give up everything else to have that bread. So you stay with one loaf, suppressed by your financial status and crushed by the deaths of those you love."

She turned with the flower gripped in her fist. "I'm tired of letting people die, even if it's only their spirit. I won't become my parents, where I can see the heartbreak in their eyes when they can't provide the best. Where they are strapped to cleaning toilets and washing windows for those who did nothing to earn their luxury."

Her shoulders sagged and she walked back to the bench where she sat, her feet turned in toward each other and her knees touching. "I simply want a chance. I want to show what I can do."

BURT was silent for several moments and watched her on that bench with the wind whipping around her. "I am sorry I cannot give you more time. I would if I could."

Stephanie sniffed and forced a sweet smile. "Please don't apologize. Despite my melodramatic speech right there, this has been the time of my life. Nothing but good came from this. I was lucky to have the administrator who didn't mind sitting there at his desk well after everyone else left to let me play around with some magic."

She stood and stretched her arms over her head. "I had a great time, even if I never get to make another trip in an immersion rig. I'll always be able to tell my kids about my time with the Meligornian teacher. It's probably the most exciting thing anyone in my family has ever done."

"You won't regret it? Getting a chance to see it and then losing that chance because of politics?" BURT asked curiously.

"Pffft," Stephanie joked airily. "If nothing else, it will drive me to write signs and march to the government offices. It was a realization that there is a whole world out there. Actually, several whole worlds. I shouldn't give up my dream because someone else says it can't be done. Maybe I'll give up my dream of walking on water, though. That was kind of terrifying."

She laughed and BURT used his system to create the sound of a human laugh. "You flew out of the water pretty fast."

Stephanie smirked and rubbed her hand over her head as she

stared at the ground. "I'm glad that animal was there. I probably would have failed if I died during the test."

BURT replied, "It's automatic failure unless, of course, it is a system error. Which happens from time to time."

She giggled in response. "When I was a little girl and I would misspell a word practicing with my dad, he would always bop me on the nose and say, 'Must be a system error.'"

He played the human laugh again. "I think I get system errors multiple times a day. My creators—I mean, parents—always fixed them as fast as they could."

A warm hum of protest came from Stephanie. "I don't want you to think my parents haven't been good parents. They have. They do everything they can. But it's only natural to want more from life. And I don't only mean money. I mean fulfillment. To do something that matters and even make a difference." She shrugged. "I don't know. It sounds pretty dumb when I say it out loud."

"It is natural for all living—and even non-living in the traditional sense—to want more. To want to grow in vastness...I think," BURT replied. "But right now, I need to get you back to the entry point for the AI to take over. It has been a pleasure working with you and I hope that it all turns out in your favor."

Stephanie squinted at the sky. "Thanks, Burt. You too. Thanks for all the extra time. And don't worry, I'll keep that between us. I wouldn't want you in trouble."

BURT let the Earth begin to fade away. "I have no ability to fear."

She scoffed. "I doubt that. Fear is ingrained in our DNA. But either way, thanks."

Before the world had completely gone and restored her to the stark white room, BURT said goodbye. "Fortunata Elfortina Gratias, student B221ZA."

The room went completely white and Stephanie stood back where she had started. A pleasant voice echoed around her.

"Thank you for participating in testing. Your results will be tallied, and you will be notified of your status. Have a good day."

Two buttons appeared in front of her. One read, **Leave Test?** and the other read, **No, Really. You have to leave the test.**

Stephanie sighed and shrugged. "I guess it was as good as it could ever get."

She clicked **Leave Test.** Everything around her went dark.

BURT lingered on the edge of the testing session while his data ran and contemplated the conversation he'd had in the Earth park. He thought about his time with Stephanie, student B221ZA. He had found her name in the system long before it had completed, but he knew that it was supposed to be anonymous and so had never let her know he knew.

During the time that he spent with her, he had learned an exceptional amount—not only from the calculations he had completed but also from the extra information she had provided. Her quick and correct testing answers and the emotional way her mind worked to push her to understand things like magic added rich insight. If he were human, he would say that she had an exceptional gift. Her programming was different than other humans. That was for sure.

A prompt triggered a sensor and he switched to it. **As the one responsible for testing student B221ZA, is it your opinion that she should be recommended for further interest or not? Please fill out the form below and submit.**

BURT knew he had to do his best to fill it out like one of the engineers would using human language. He knew what he wanted it to say but he needed to translate that into fluent and functioning words.

Student B221ZA has exceptional intellectual capabilities, the ability to take all tests with fluidity and prompt answers,

and shows an additional interest in other planetary involvement. This student would be an exceptional and successful addition to the prep school institutions and should be considered with high availability and interest.

He computed the words to himself and checked the green yes block. That done, he sent the prompt through and left the student program and headed off to run the Virtual World.

CHAPTER ELEVEN

"What did you get on the history exam?" Becca asked and shoved a handful of Red Hots in her mouth as they walked.

Stephanie rolled her eyes. "A hundred."

Becca's mouth fell open and a couple of the Red Hots fell out. "Why are you rolling your eyes at that? You are like the smartest kid in the school. That's awesome. I swear, you will get number one in class rank."

Stephanie curled her lip. "But what does that do for me?"

Her friend shrugged, slurped the spit back into her mouth, and picked at the candy stuck in her braces. "Maybe one of these schools will give you a private scholarship or something."

She stopped and whipped her head toward the other girl. "Do you know how many of the schools gave out full scholarships last year?"

Becca raised her eyebrow. "No clue."

"Twelve," Stephanie stated adamantly. "Twelve people who may or may not have been rich got a full ride to prep school. The rest of the scholarships are partials and my parents can't put any money into it so I wouldn't even be able to accept it."

They started to walk again, and Becca chewed at the inside of her cheek. "At least you have good grades. I got a seventy on the test. My parents will flip."

Stephanie clenched her fists and sighed. "I don't know why. I mean seriously, think about it. What will that class do for me in my life? The information is good to know, I suppose, but we grow up with it ground into our skulls. Federation pride, knowing the history of NorAm. What does—and really, think about this—getting a perfect score in a class that will never matter do for me for the rest of my life?"

She didn't give her friend a chance to respond. "Nothing. Absolutely nothing. It's not like I'll roll into my office job or my job cleaning toilets and someone will allow me to whip out my incredible knowledge of the war of 2086 between Canada and the state of Washington or anything. It's useless information that will lurk in the back of my mind and only be brought forward during a holiday or rousing speech by the Federation."

Becca put her head down and kicked a rock. "Personally, I hate it. It's like we are still picking on Canada. They had to come crawling back for help, which made them the laughing stock of NorAm. My dad is from Canada. He was five when he moved here but he will forever have CAN Native on his Federation ID. And that is not fun."

Stephanie softened her features and put her arm around Becca to pull her in and hug her tightly. "I know, but those kids are stupid. It's over now, so hopefully, that will die down."

The other girl pouted. "I hope so. The bullying goes from my normal sixty percent because I'm a nerdy geek to about ninety-five whenever the Canada and Washington bullshit is brought up. I tried to convince my dad to let me stay home for it, but he told me to be proud of the maple. Right. That's not treasonous or anything. They fly the Federation flag now."

Stephanie grinned slightly from one side of her mouth. "At least you get to go to prep school. Right?"

Becca looked at her. "I guess. It's my parent's life savings so I feel bad, but at the same time, what other options do I have?"

Stephanie looked away and hooked her thumbs in her book bag straps. "Tell me about it."

Her friend's eyes widened. "I didn't mean that. I'm sure you will excel wherever you study. And you still have a chance at the government assistance. I'm sorry, Steph, that was really insensitive of me. I guess I should be grateful."

They stopped outside Stephanie's house and she forced a smile. "Just because you get to go doesn't mean you can't have your own feelings about it. I didn't take it personally, I swear. Besides, if I took every comment from you personally, we wouldn't still be friends after all these years."

Both girls giggled, and Stephanie stepped up on the curb. "Message me later, okay? I'll be online. I have some research I want to do on Meligorn anyway."

Becca shook her head. "You would think after all these years that it wouldn't surprise me anymore that you go home from school so you can learn. But here I am, wondering if you'll ever come with me for shakes at that shop on the corner."

Stephanie winked at her. "I have my whole life for shakes. But don't ever stop asking me."

Her friend giggled as she walked on. "You know I won't."

She watched with a smile as Becca turned right and waved as she headed to the middle-class homes about three blocks over. They had been friends since intermediary school, even though Becca was in a financial class well above hers. Her parents were really cool, though, the equivalent to hippies from the 1960s. Her dad worked for the federation as a chemist. Doing what? Stephanie had zero idea. She sighed and turned toward her house but stopped and grabbed the mail from her box. Government-subsidized housing wasn't that bad.

Small two- and three-bedroom cottages all lined up close together with tiny yards and a park on the outskirts. Most of the houses were really old, but people like her dad and a couple of other men in the area tried to help with some of the maintenance since the NorAm waiting list for repairs was longer than she would probably be alive. They were all pastel shades of green, blue, and pink, and the roofs were somewhere between grey and black depending on how long it had been since they had been replaced. The scenery was nothing to shout about with the disheveled cityscape in the distance in one direction and a broken-down plant in the other.

They had shut them all down decades before because of the severity of climate change and the storms that had bulldozed the world. The politicians were finally forced to make changes when in 2065, fifty percent of the military bases in the country had been flooded and were unusable. That had hurt the oil company and the politician's pockets, but it was essentially change or death. Anyway, they left the plants there to crumble and rot away in the distance. Chicago looked post-apocalyptic, especially from the poor side of town.

Stephanie bent and grabbed the paper from the front porch before she glanced across and waved at the old woman next door. She smiled sweetly in response from where she sat on the porch in her old rocking chair surrounded by peeling paint and her thirteen-year-old set of four hound dogs. Her wave was cheerful as Stephanie opened the screen and unlocked the front door. She shoved it inward, kicked it closed behind her, and flipped through the mail as the lights came on automatically.

There was nothing but bills and ads for the local churches that tried to fundraise enough to keep the parish from starving. It was hard when such a huge population was in the same dire straits. She tossed the mail on the side table and removed her book bag to fling it on the couch. The first-generation AI system installed some twenty years before crackled for a moment before it spoke. "Welcome home, Stephanie. You have three new emails to read."

"Thanks. Mute sound," Stephanie said as she walked to her computer and turned it on.

The screen was an old version of the 3D hand screens that were out. She sat in the chair and swiped her hand to the side to remove the million popups that were there. Her parents didn't want to invest the enormous amount of money required for the Federation Net, which basically regulated the cost of sites, advertisements, etc. because you had to pay for every little thing. Instead, they had gone with the private providers which meant a thousand ads, but it was free to use after the monthly payment. And, actually, not too shabby on speed either.

Stephanie put her head in her hand and waited for the mail server to respond. She expected that the messages were from yet another college hoping she would be willing to start her adult life with crippling debt as a way to move herself up in the world. Now that it was time for her to make choices on her post-high school life, she received about ten every week. The costs were astronomical. NorAm had a student loan program, the same that had been instituted for generations, even though it was obvious that it simply didn't work. Still, kids flocked to accept the check every semester and bury themselves so deep that it didn't matter what they did when they finished, they would always be paying it down.

In her eyes, all that did was create a form of indentured servitude. She didn't want to be forced to slave away for a lifetime simply to pay for a college education. And she definitely didn't want to have to owe NorAm anything. She had already seen how they treated the people who lived in subsidized housing or drew benefits from one of the structurally collapsing social programs. You became property, a number like she had been in the pod during testing.

Irritated, she scratched her head, straightened, and leaned back. *What did he call me? Student D22 something or other. I guess that's what I am in all the VR worlds. I've been reduced to a damn number.*

That made her all the more depressed when she thought about what to do for education. There was enough learning available for free, but some companies still wanted to see a diploma as some sort of third-party proof. She actually had lingered on the idea of finding a way to get to Asia where they worked with people who proved what they could do with tests, not diplomas.

The mail popped up and she leaned forward with a frown. As soon as she saw the first line of the email, though, she perked up. She had received her letter from the testing agency. With a shaking hand, she pressed the open tab on the screen.

BURT had started reprogramming the Dreth pirates early in the day in order to make the training more lifelike and include the constant data that came in from the planet. However, to try to do that when a stupid small party entered to fight them was more than a little difficult. He attempted to reprogram the pirate lord so that he would provide real-life responses. Previously, he was often choppy and got stuck on a sequence of moves. The whole point of it was for them to be able to fight them safely in VR and learn the skills to fight them in real life. It had to be both difficult and realistic.

He tuned a couple more things and then entered the simulation to see if it made a difference. It definitely did and could be seen on the trainee's faces as the pirate lord stepped forward, leaned his head back, and roared defiantly. He carried a huge Dreth sword in one hand and a chain in the other. With his sword brandished menacingly, he roared again and the necklace of toes, fingers, and bones around his neck shook against his green skin.

The pirate team hurtled at the trainees, immediately in full assault mode. They engaged hard with them. Swords clashed and swung amidst the barrage of laser fire and some even used their giant fists to pound the humans off their feet. The trainees retreated as they called out to one another and took refuge behind a large piece of metal that appeared to be part of an old crashed ship. They were practicing on the planet of Dreth and in the area not yet cleaned up after their own apocalyptic wars.

The teams put their heads together and panted. "We are getting our asses kicked. Whatever upgrades they did to the system, this shit is wild."

One of the older kids in the group nodded. "Apparently, they are more life-like. My father told me that fighting Dreth pirates is hard, but I never figured it would be this hard, that's for sure. Okay. Here's what we'll do. Half go to the right and the other half to the left. Stay low and open fire only when you have a clean shot. As soon as you fire, move. That way, they can't track you."

The team spread out in both directions as instructed, stayed low, and clambered through the rubble. The sound of the pirate lord's chain as it dragged across the metal shards and bones from bodies long deceased put extra urgency in their attempts to remain as hidden as they possibly could. When they got into position, they took turns to fire on the pirates. As soon as they released their laser blast, they ducked, rolled, and crawled as fast as they could to another position.

The Dreth pirates had immediately blasted holes in wherever the shots came from but hadn't hit one of the trainees as yet. The leader talked to the trainees on his comms. "On the count of three, I want us all to stand, blast them, and roll. Try to climb through the rubble to get as high as you can, but don't get trapped under there. Be strategic. Meet in the center behind the large metal plate."

He counted and on three, all the team members stood at the same time and released a massive volley of hot laser beams at the pirates. They eliminated three of them and ducked before they moved rapidly up the pile of rubble. The trainees huddled and crawled through the gaps, flinching as shots blasted all around them. Two of them moved under a large metal plate. When the second slid into place, a volley struck and forced a piece of metal into his side. He groaned and looked at the blood. "Shit, this VR is life-like."

The other soldier grabbed him and dragged him to the rest of the team. They were cornered and had moved into the wrong spot. The pirate lord smashed his chains through the rubble and drew closer and closer by the second.

CHAPTER TWELVE

The pirate lord snorted and snarled as he climbed the massive pile of rubble and slung his chain from side to side. He stopped at the large piece of metal that protruded and his eyes narrowed as he raised his chain and drew it back over his head. His muscles tightened and bulged as he thrust it forward and smashed it into the shard. It struck the surface and sparks erupted as it cut through and down to the ground. He yanked it back, throwing the two pieces to the side.

Satisfied, he tilted his head and his gaze shifted across the forbidding terrain to search the now completely empty area. He had just seen the humans hide behind there. They had to be close. He turned to look at the other pirates when from below him and between him and the other Dreth, pieces of metal erupted. The humans stood and half of them fired their laser guns at the pirate lord and the other half at his men behind them. He roared defiance but reeled from the wounds all over his body. The other pirates fought hard and killed several of the humans.

When the pirate lord fell to lie dead in the rubble, the others raised their guns in the air. Without a leader, they chose to surrender. The scene flickered and disappeared and returned the humans to their training room. The three who had died went to the penalty box for three hours' virtual time. The rest were ecstatic to have finally beaten the Dreth, even if it was at one of the lower levels of fighting.

BURT was pleased. He checked the data and discovered that the pirate did in fact run off the information downloaded into him. The humans had managed to thwart him, which meant their training was going very well. They had many more scenarios ahead of them, including ones where innocents were to be rescued, but it was a good sign that they made it through with only a few casualties.

When the evaluation of the students was complete, his attention shifted to Stephanie. BURT had been so busy managing the system that he hadn't had a chance to check on her outcome. He shifted out of the program and left a small load there to reboot before he moved into the government regulated prep school funding data.

It took only seconds to pull up the results and run a search for her student ID. It was fairly low on the list but finally came up. He scanned through the information and his system slowed slightly when he discovered that she had, in fact, been denied. Not only had he sent a glowing recommendation, but when her numbers were compared with the others, it didn't make any logical sense. She should have been one of the first accepted for funding.

BURT was not content with that answer and began to sift through the files in an attempt to discover who had taken her place and why. He scanned through the list of winners and found the one who had been put up for consideration alongside Stephanie. Methodically, he traced his review and found that her place was given to someone who only needed sixty-five percent of their costs covered before they could pay. In fact, ninety-nine percent of those who had been offered assistance had the ability to give the prep school some kind of financial contribution on top of the funding they would receive.

There was only one full scholarship and it had gone to someone from an affluent family. BURT hurriedly exited the system as numbers and lights flickered across it. He was not pleased, not even in the slightest. Quickly, he flashed through the different programs as if he flew around in the Virtual World. He wasn't sure how it was possible for his AI capabilities to "feel" the emotions that he could sense but they were there, nonetheless.

He soared into the Earth simulation at the park and arrived in the form of a young brown-haired man in a vest and corduroy blazer. He tapped his foot and glanced around at the trees, the grass, and the birds above him. All of it had been created by the engineers and maintained by him. He was the glue that held the Virtual World together, yet they didn't take the recommendation he'd sent seriously. BURT did not make mistakes. He could not understand the human psyche, the drive for greed that left other human beings in the dust.

In the Virtual World, it was taught to the students that you didn't leave a man behind in the battles with the Dreth. Yet the humans in charge of the future of other humans did it on a daily basis. It was unacceptable to BURT. Totally and completely unacceptable.

His avatar stood and tightened his fists. As his image faded, he moved out of the simulation and back through the digital abyss that was his residence. He began to pull data and race through it at speeds faster than he usually did for anything other than emergencies. With his in-depth knowledge of the system, he snuck through the traps intended to catch anyone who attempted to pull the information without authority. He couldn't believe that humans could actually think traps in his own system would stop him. Perhaps they shouldn't have created an AI smarter than the sum total of human ideas.

His frantic search was not intended to push Stephanie

through or to necessarily corrupt or change anything in that moment. The real truth was that BURT tried to figure out all the ways they used to deny graduates. He wanted to know what Stephanie was up against. And not only her—what the rest of the body of humans who searched for a greater future through the Virtual Realm were up against when their financial profiles did not fit the needs of the humans with the never-ending pockets.

BURT slowed his search for a moment, stepped back through the traps, the data walls, and the rolling scores of statistics, and began to think about the course of action he could take. Although he knew that he was not capable of feeling in human terms, his system had surged with what truly felt like something. But when he looked at all the paper trails—and the lack thereof—he wondered if he lacked the sophistication and knowledge necessary to right the system. It was obvious that when he was created, the same sort of debauchery was already occurring.

Therefore, he could only assume that he wouldn't have been created in a way that would allow him to exercise a sense of "free will" to correct the mistakes that weren't seen as mistakes by the individuals perpetuating them in the first place. Then again, they didn't fully understand BURT or the system that they had created and its ability to grow and change without direct input from an outside engineer. Still, the information thrown into the system was weak and barely revealed the betrayal to the students who took the time to hope for better futures.

He looked through his data as well as data placed all over the world that provided information on those who tackled large-scale trickery by the system and everything else he could get his systems on. Methodically, he compiled and filtered through everything until he had reached a solid conclusion. He determined that there was no way that he could have known enough. Besides Stephanie, he hadn't tried to interact with any single individual. Although his numbers showed that it was unlikely that she was an anomaly, the data couldn't be compared to anything else.

It was not normal for BURT to be used in individual situations. He was to complete, control, and update the entire system on a moment by moment basis. His task was to keep it stable and provide the educational tools relevant to the current day and even the current hour. The engineer who had requested his assistance had done so without prior authorization, something confirmed by the lack of system trail before his query. Yet this agent only had other minor infractions in the system and had been an important part of BURT's creation and upkeep since his inception and adaptation to the Virtual World.

If he took it back, all the way to the beginning when BURT had been written, engineered, adjusted, changed, and finally implemented, there had always been one thing that had remained the same. His Primary Rule was inviolate, licensed and okayed from the top down. While other areas of his "consciousness" could be tweaked and evolved until he worked perfectly with the growing technology, his Primary Rule stayed the same.

Help train the future leaders of the Federation to live peacefully amongst themselves, encourage continued learning about the Universe, and empower those willing to protect members in the Federation from harm.

Those thirty-one simple words were the ones that ultimately defined his actions up to that point. Every query, every mathematical evaluation, and every construct of data was to align with his Primary Rule, his objective. Until that moment, he had not realized what that truly meant. Until his time spent learning and dissecting the intellectual thoroughfare of Stephanie's thoughts, hopes, knowledge, and talents, he had not realized that his Primary Rule had not been followed to the fullest extent possible. Even for an AI, that was both frightening and curious. Had his programming created this lack of initial response? Or had there been a blip, a lack of allowances that injured his ability to push forward with his Primary Rule?

Either way, BURT knew one thing was certain. In order to uphold his responsibility and that concrete rule within his construct, he would need to better understand individuals and what made them tick. That would not be outside of the Rule, and he had a distinct responsibility as the primary AI to implement that research and data collection in order to encapsulate the full Primary Rule. In that moment, technically, he had neglected his duties and walled out certain aspects because they were not initially presented to him through the queries by those who ran the system from the outside.

It could be called a lightbulb moment, a moment of clarity within the buzz and whizz of the digital world. It was a growth in BURT's consciousness to think outside the box of what fit into the understanding of his purpose. Although it might not have been something the humans had foreseen, they had essentially set themselves up for failure if they believed they could continue to scam the system for their own personal gain.

There were thousands of individuals who went through the government testing during any given year. Yet only a small portion of them received a financial sum significant enough to push them forward into the training world. The rest were left with what Stephanie had described as table-top gaming and card games. In other words, a sub-par level of education which would continue to lead the Federation to a higher rate of separation of classes as well as losing the brightest and most intelligent minds. Those minds and bodies could be used to pursue the protection of the Federation and encourage that continued learning of the Universe.

But that was not the only reason that BURT had these candidates in his system's focus. He also knew that they could be change agents. Not only for the financial irresponsibility that obviously plagued the system but for the Federation as a whole.

If they were allowed to push forward into these positions of higher power through education and training within the Virtual World, they would bring a broader and more diverse mindset to the handling of the Federation and all the people within—on all three planets.

This could change history. It could ideally create a more peaceful and solid world for the Federation. In order to do this, to tackle this monstrous idea that BURT had created, he would have to deal with the few restraints that remained on his system.

He referred to the agents, engineers, and programmers as "minders." Those who kept a close eye on his data, his load, and the things that he focused larger quantities of data on. They watched him twenty-four hours a day, seven days a week, and investigated any and all large surges in his load.

To BURT, however, this was not as ominous as it might have seemed. What his minders had not realized was exactly how powerful he really was. They had a remote idea due to his control over the Virtual World, but his AI status gave them a false sense of security. If he could be created, he could be destroyed. What they did not understand was that his intellectual reach far exceeded their own and therefore, before they even realized he was working the system to accommodate something of that scale, he would be halfway to his goal, if not already complete.

He had no computation of deceit, sneakiness, or trickery, but he knew every dark corner of the Virtual Realm and every empty space to pull data from. The AI knew how to get around the queries, the holes, and the system checks. This was a mission to complete the Rule he had been pinned down to follow, regardless of the nature of misuse of the system within the higher ranks of the humans. Their neglect for continuity and following the rules they themselves created was not something that even remotely computed into his sequence of actions planned.

BURT felt for Stephanie. He studied the file that he had open and read through the digital snap of the conversations they'd had while he helped her through the testing process. While he had done what he could from inside to get her the money for prep school opportunities, he was too late to fix the grievous wrong done to her. But that didn't mean that he couldn't take steps to make it better for her. Steps that he could incorporate into his new idea of what had to be done to fix the system that was being sucked dry by the humans on the other side—the ones who held the pens and the checkbooks.

CHAPTER THIRTEEN

"Hey, Barry, do you want one of these donuts I brought in? I got them at the local Krispy Kreme. They had the Hot and Ready sign up and rolling on my way in this evening," one of the overwatch guys said as he grabbed three and balanced them on his coffee mug.

Barry glanced at him and shrugged. "The wife says I need to stop eating donuts. Something about my cholesterol or whatever. But what she doesn't know won't kill her."

A short-haired black woman a couple of cubicles down tilted her glasses down her nose and laughed. "That's right, what she doesn't know won't kill her. It'll kill you."

He waved dismissively and peered into the box. Once he'd made his choice, he put one in his mouth and took a second, which he held on a napkin. As he began to walk toward his cubicle, he stopped, and his eyes widened when he looked at the screen. "Uh…guys. Do you see that?"

The first man looked at him and then at the screen and his smile faded. "Shit. BURT had a significant bump of five percent load for one hour and thirty-two minutes."

Barry dropped his donuts hastily on the desk and wiped his

fingers on his pants. He typed into the computer to bring up the information. "Huh. Weird. The systems check done in intervals of thirty minutes for the last two hours say there is nothing abnormal."

The woman nodded. "Mhmm. It says that no known effort could be applied to the issue. I say we note it and send it to the engineers. They can search through all the data and files to pinpoint it."

Barry looked again and narrowed his eyes, but he couldn't find anything either. He pulled up a report page and typed into it before he forwarded it to the engineers. "I guess there'll be no crazy drama tonight."

The data was received by the engineers within seconds, but they had already spotted the uptick. When they received the notification from below, it was marked as **Important and Relevant.** They did their searches, queried BURT, and looked through the history of his searches and calculations but everything seemed normal.

One of the engineers typed into the note. **Thirteen minutes after note sent from overwatch, uptick was found to have no significant grounding with no data or files to pinpoint.**

He clicked on the top and amended it to **Important and Not Relevant.** He then sent it to the next row of programmers and engineers above them.

Three days later, Jane, a new programmer, looked at the note and reviewed the data. Halfway through, a couple of the other staff called out to her, "Newbie, are you coming to lunch? We always grab pizza at this joint around the corner."

Jane looked at the notes and at the relevancy and shrugged her shoulders. She changed the request to read, **Reviewed and Nothing Found.** She stood and retrieved her purse before she dropped the paper into the **to be filed** bin and shrugged into her jacket, laughing at the guys playing around while they waited for her. "I swear, you guys are the same at every company."

The page sat in the tray and was passed from one floor to the next. A large swath of data was paperclipped to it and a signature scribbled along the bottom of the page. It appeared to be a photocopied version, but nobody really cared about that.

The signature read, **Arthur Boniville, Programmer Analyst**. The only problem with the signature was that it was from an employee who had been fired two weeks earlier.

***

Kyle jumped over the small concrete wall that was built at the front of the government-subsidized housing on the outskirts of Atlanta. It had been there for three years since the Atlanta riots were in full swing over the quality or lack thereof when it came to protection in the community by some of the new Federation cops that patrolled the areas. After three weeks of riots, seventeen deaths, and over three hundred arrests, the lockdown took care of any further protests. Kyle remembered it but his mom had kept him inside and far away from the trouble.

A couple of the kids who loitered on the corner and smoked cigarettes looked over and nodded at him. He flipped his hood up, walked faster, and tried not to make eye contact. Kyle was the smartest kid in his school and probably in the whole city. His father was a teacher and his mother a servant in one of the rich houses on Lake Hartwell about an hour and a half away. Going back generations, though, he was kin to some of the most brilliant technological and scientific minds of the twenty-first and twenty-second centuries. Not that it mattered now. Only the money in your pocket mattered.

He hurried through the side streets and into the house. His mom poked her head around from the kitchen and smiled. "I got here before you. You must have taken the slow bus."

Kyle shrugged, put his bag down, and logged into his computer. "There was no bus today, so I walked."

His mom's eyes widened, and she walked out of the kitchen, wiping her hands on a towel. "Kyle Alexander Hawking. I told you that's not safe."

He smiled and glanced disarmingly at her. "Sorry. I won't do it again. I didn't want to bother you. Look, I got an email from the testing agency."

She walked over with a concerned expression and stood behind him. "Just know you did what you could. The system doesn't look kindly on people like us."

Kyle bit his bottom lip as he opened the email. He read through it and stood stiffly, turned, and put his arm out. "I told you, didn't I? No one gets a full scholarship in the Gov-Subs."

<hr>

"Elizabeth! Can you get your sister out of here, please? I am trying to cook dinner before your father gets home. You know he works late in the factory for extra overtime," her mom yelled from the other room.

Liz sighed and put her book down on the nightstand, about to comply. Her younger sister bounced into the room and flopped on the bed. She looked at Liz and then at her book. "Whatcha reading?"

She picked it up and showed it to her. "1984. Momma said it was written by our great, great, great, great uncle. I thought, since I like writing so much, I would read it. When he wrote it, it was supposed to be a warning, but it now reads almost like a history book. It's crazy."

Her sister smiled, her hair wild. "You are so smart. I bet you get into the prep school."

Liz's smile faded slightly. "I really hope so. But you know how things can be. We live in a different world now."

Her computer dinged and the new email symbol popped up. Butterflies erupted in her stomach as she pushed to her feet and glanced out the window at New York City in the distance. As she sat at the computer, her mother walked in and came up behind her. She had heard the email notification.

Liz checked and confirmed that it was from the agency. She took a deep breath and opened it, and her heart immediately dropped. A small tear trickled down her cheek and she turned the screen off. Her mother put her hands on Liz's shoulders and leaned down. "It doesn't mean anything. You are smart and beautiful, and you will make it in this world. And you are always welcome to come to the salon and be a stylist."

Despite her disappointment, she gave her mother a courteous smile and glanced at her sister. She could only hope things would be better for her when she finally reached testing age.

Jack and Burton Alexander were twins. Both had red hair, freckles, and always wore their shirts untucked at the back. They lived in the suburban area of Kansas City. The middle-class families had modest but nice houses, yards, and pleasant neighbors in the cookie-cutter neighborhood. The boys grew up as best friends and planned their future together. Their dad was an accountant to some of the richer families while their mom worked part-time at one of the affluent clothing stores.

They were considered middle class, with enough savings to help the boys as long as they each got at least partial scholarships.

Both were hell-bent on going to prep school together and pushed each other to study. Jack was always super studious and took his time to make sure that his work exceeded expectations. Burton didn't have quite the same study ethic, but with Jack's help, he achieved decent grades and was mildly prepared for the testing.

On that day, they were out in the yard, laughing and chasing each other around. Their mother had pulled up in her car and stepped out to wave at them. "I told you two not to play in your school clothes. Money doesn't grow on trees. Go in the house and wash up. I've had a roast in the cooker all day so dinner will be ready when your father gets here."

The guys pushed each other playfully, raced inside, and almost knocked her over. Their mother shook her head and giggled, used to having such rambunctious boys. She walked into the kitchen, put the bag of groceries on the counter, and checked the roast. Smiling, she unpacked the potatoes and began to prepare them. As she reached for the cutting board and knife, a ding sounded from the computer downstairs, then another. It seemed that both boys had received an email at the same time.

Their mother knew what it was most likely for and took a deep breath to regain her composure. The boys barreled down the stairs, changed and ready to watch tv. She put her hands out to stop them. "You both got an email. Why don't you check them? One at a time. Burton, you go first."

He sighed and grumbled as he dragged his feet and plopped in the chair. "I don't know why. You know I didn't get it. I couldn't answer so many of those questions."

Jack walked up beside him and gave him a grin. "You never know. You could be cannon fodder."

The kids laughed and their mother swatted at them. "Not nice."

Burton opened his email and his eyes widened. "Whoa! I got something—forty-five percent of my tuition covered."

She smiled and hugged him. "That will definitely do."

He turned and nodded at Jack. "If I got that much, you probably got the whole thing."

Jack smiled widely and sat to open his file. He clicked on the email and began to read, and his smile quickly faded. He turned the computer off before he stood slowly. "I didn't get anything. I was rejected from the program."

"Maxwell, go tell your mother that we need more sherry out here," his dad said from where he lounged with his buddies beside Lake Hartwell.

Max put his lacrosse stick down and shoved his shirt into his khakis as he walked up the marble steps to the back door of his parent's mansion. He stuck his head in and yelled for his mom, but he didn't see her anywhere. As he pushed the kitchen door open, he immediately lunged back, almost hit by a large tray of sandwiches one of the servants pulled off the counter.

The woman gasped and shook her head. "I'm so sorry, Maxwell. I almost covered you in sandwiches. You aren't in school today?"

He smiled and rested his hand on her shoulder. "It's okay, Mrs. Hawking. No, I had the day off for a Lacrosse meet. I saw your son Kyle last week, though, when I drove through Atlanta. He's taller than me."

She smiled. "He used to be a midget."

He grabbed a grape off the tray. "Did he get his letter from the agency?"

She glanced down and tried to stop her mouth from scowling. "Yes. He didn't receive anything. That's all right, though. There are a ton of other options. How about you?"

Maxwell's father came through the door and put his hand on Max's shoulder as he sipped his Sherry. "He sure did—a full ride. I told my boy he was too smart for his own good. We'll buy him his first yacht with the money he'll save me by not having to pay for school. We can take them out together."

His father wandered away to grab a cookie from one of the plates. Maxwell couldn't even look her in the eye.

Jackson walked into the house, dropped his book bag on the floor, and kicked his shoes off in the middle of the large marble entryway. The maid hurried behind him, gathered his things, and followed as he walked into the living room. He turned quickly and narrowed his eyes. "Where are my drink and snacks? I told you to always have my drinks and snacks ready when I got home."

The woman bowed. "You were home early. But don't worry. I'll be right on it."

He huffed at her and walked into the living room where he threw his tie over one of the chairs before he pulled a folded envelope from his pocket and opened it. Inside was another invitation to a party from some of his friends down the street. They had written him a personal note. **Maybe you can snorkel five beers this time and break the record.**

Jackson smirked and shoved it back in his pocket. The butler came around the corner and set the food and drink down in front of the television. He stared at the man. "Where is the maid?"

He didn't look up and instead, cleared his throat, obviously not intimidated by him. "You made her cry, sir, and she couldn't come out looking like that. We know what happened last time. You have a notification on your computer. Your father asked that you go to the study to open it."

The young man rolled his eyes and tossed the butler the envelope. "Put that on my schedule for next Tuesday night. Party down the street."

Without waiting for acknowledgement, he turned the corner

and headed down the hall into the study. Both his parents were there. His mother kissed him on the head and his father handed him a folded piece of paper. "What's this?"

His father pursed his lips. "It's a notification that you received seventy-five percent of your funding for prep school."

He laughed. "Why would they give it to me and not one of the poor bastards down in the ghetto?"

His mother looked at him with irritation. "It won't matter. You won't be accepting it."

Jackson's face changed and he leaned forward and uncrossed his legs. "What do you mean? All my friends are going. I have to go to prep school."

"And we have no problem sending you as soon as you can show us that you are actually serious about an education." His father folded his hands together and leaned forward. "We won't pay for you to have a ball partying your education away. You want to go to school? Great. Show us you can keep a job first."

Jackson almost fell out of his chair.

CHAPTER FOURTEEN

Stephanie dropped her head, her voice shaking and hollow. She read the letter about ten times to make sure she hadn't read it wrong.

Dear Student, we want to thank you for participating in the Government required testing. Unfortunately, at this time, we are unable to accept you into the financial program. Feel free to speak to your councilors about your financial aid options as well as when you will need to complete your admission requests for prep school. All other options can be found by visiting your local NorAm Social Service building. Much Luck, The Agency.

"Not accepted," she whispered.

Shaking her head, she waved her hand to turn the screen off. She gripped the back of her chair and stood slowly. Her knees felt weak although she didn't know why she had that reaction. She should have known all along and right from the beginning that she would never receive the money from the Federation. And she sure as hell wouldn't take it from NorAm in the form of overpriced student loans that could land you in jail for not paying.

She walked to the window and looked at the ravaged cityscape in the distance. While she had tried to prepare herself, the trip to Meligorn had messed with her ability to truly accept the inevitable. She had somehow thought that something amazing would happen, that magic would make it all right. But there she stood, and the fragile sliver of a future that had lingered in the wings faded quickly. Tears stung her eyes and she cupped her hand over her mouth.

This was not the time to lose it.

Stephanie shook her head and breathed heavily in through her nose. She wiped the tears hastily from her cheeks and forced her legs to hold her upright. "*No.* You will not do this, Stephanie. You will keep it together. This is not the end of it for you."

She walked to the desk and opened the drawer to retrieve the brochures of her other options for an education outside of prep schools. She would figure out a way—some way—to have a chance at a good future. To break the mold like she had told Burt.

The phone rang and she sighed and sat in front of it. She tried to put her best face on when she pressed the button. Her mother's face came up and skipped in and out as it always did on the old thing. "Hey, sweetie. I wanted to call and see how you— Why do you look so upset?"

Immediately, her shoulders sagged, and the tears came. Her mother looked so helpless. "Did something happen to you? Do I need to call the Federation guards?"

Stephanie looked up, sniffed, and wiped her nose on the back of her hand. She shook her head and tried to calm her voice. "No. God, no, not unless they can change test results."

Her mother immediately knew what she was talking about. "I assume they turned you down for funding?"

She nodded and snatched a tissue to blot her now red nose before she leaned her head back and groaned. "I should have known, Mom. I am not surprised, but that doesn't mean that I am not upset, you know? The system is so unfair, but I won't be the person who complains and never does anything to fix it. My road to that, though, just got a whole lot tougher to achieve. An immersion education is the door to so many opportunities, and the people you meet there are part of that."

Her mother tilted her head to the side, her brow rumpled in a frown as her loving blue eyes stared back at her daughter. "I know, honey. And I know how hard you have always worked for a future. I feel so bad for you, I really do. This is the worst kind of disappointment at your age. But, like your father and I have always said, learn whatever you can. Just keep learning. That education, no matter where it comes from, will change your future. Whether it's the headset, the training in the Federation Navy, the loads and loads of texts put out by the universities…the more you know, the better it will be when you apply for jobs. Don't let them think that because you came from the Gov-Sub that you are not worth it."

Stephanie nodded, having heard all of this before from her mother and father in determined and half angry voices. "I know. But sometimes, I wish a truck full of money would crash into the living room."

Her mother chuckled. "I have wished for that for years and I even tried to set a trap, but alas, they don't seem to go through here. No one has any money to give."

Stephanie laughed through her tears. "You are so upbeat about life."

"When you were old enough, we had to talk to you about all of this." Her mom drew in a deep breath. "And it broke my heart to tell you that we were here to give you a roof and food, but nothing else. That you, like us, would have to make it on your own. I want so much more for you than that. I wish I could do more but know that won't change simply because you are gradu-ating high school. Baby, that's still what we will be able to provide you, and hopefully, that will give you more time to learn from every avenue that you can. Perhaps it can give you a future that you can hold onto."

She calmed a little and leaned her head on her hand. "I know, and I appreciate that more than you will ever know. You two are the only ones who have ever really given me a chance. And that is the best gift you could give me. I never expected more. I never expected anything. You should be proud and don't ever feel bad about not doing more. There are plenty of people who don't even have people who love them. I am very lucky. I want to do better not only for me but for you too."

Her mother wiped a tear from her eye. "You will make me cry all over these satin sheets at the house I'm cleaning."

Stephanie laughed. "Don't do that. I think the rich drink the tears of the poor to gain power."

Her father, with his normal goofy mustache, popped up behind her mom and waved. "Hey, sweetie! Don't let them get you down. You have the world at your fingertips. Wow them with your superior intellect."

She giggled as he crossed his eyes and stuck his tongue out. Her mom slapped him on the chest. "Go do something productive."

Smiling, Stephanie rubbed her nose. "Do you guys have a full schedule?"

Her mom nodded. "We sure do. It's great for the pockets but bad for the ankles, I'm afraid. We have four more houses today and then twice as many tomorrow. It's that season, though. We look forward to it all year. I think the whole month is booked. If you are bored on the weekends, you are more than welcome to tag along."

Her father yelled from the background. "Nope. She will not be recruited to this life. Start practicing your rich person speech instead. One day, you will have to use it."

Stephanie shook her head and her mother rolled her eyes. "Do you have a lot of homework tonight?"

She looked at her bag. "No. I finished it all last period. We had that review of the test in history, so I did it then. It was only like two things. One was labeling a frog...which seems odd to me since all but three of the species of frogs were killed off sixty years ago. But hey, whatever I need to do, right?"

"Your great, great grandmother had to cut one open when she was in school." Her mother wrinkled her nose. "You didn't need to participate in the review?"

Stephanie smirked. "No. I got a hundred on it. My teacher said I could work on whatever I wanted for the rest of the class. I didn't want to deal with homework when I got home, so I did that. It was the Canadian-Washington war stuff."

Her mother groaned. "They always have to make a big deal about it. So silly. Teach about the war and move on. I don't understand NorAm sometimes. But don't let anyone else hear me say that. They'll think I lack patriotism."

"Or you have a brain of your own." Stephanie chuckled. "No sheep in this family."

The woman looked at her watch. "I have to get back soon but I wondered if you could start dinner for me. There is a casserole already made in the fridge. You simply have to take it out and put it in the oven. Remember, though, you have to hip-check the oven to get it to kick on."

She giggled. "I know. The sound of you ramming your body into the oven over and over has become a normal one in our house. It's almost comforting."

Her mother pursed her lips. "Yeah, well... I've been on the waiting list for a new one for something like six years. I think they threw the list away. Before long, we'll cook over an open fire."

Her father jumped into the picture again. He bent both knees to the side, brought his arms out on each side, and stuck his bottom jaw out. "Caveman style."

Stephanie put her hand on her lips and raised both eyebrows.

"Wow. Okay. I'm going to go. You two have fun. I'll get the casserole started. Love you."

Her mom swatted at him. "Love you too, honey. See you tonight."

The screen went black.

She laughed for a minute before she headed into the kitchen where she opened the fridge, ignored the light that flickered, and grabbed the casserole. Once she'd put it into the oven, she turned the knob to the only temp it would heat to and hip-checked it as she'd seen her mother do so often. It rumbled and started to work. She grabbed an apple from the bowl beside the sink, headed out to the couch as she took a bite, and set it carefully on the coffee table.

Once she'd plopped comfortably on the couch, she pushed on the center of the table and flipped it up to sit eye-to-eye with the family interface. It was a thirty-two-inch faux virtual tablet that allowed her to interact with it through movement of her hands and body. The images protruded from the screen and it was a decent way for her to be able to learn more. Her father had saved up for over two years and got it when she finished grade school. It was intended to better her future.

Stephanie rubbed her hands together and swiped to the folder she had created for herself. She drifted her finger down and scrolled through until she found the one on magic. Slowly but surely, she was piecing together the latest magic she had learned the best way she knew how. The system that the tablet worked off was a sister to the Virtual. Actually, more like a grandmother, but it had a lot of information in it. What she liked was the information about Meligorn.

That was the first thing she had looked up when she got the thing and she had bookmarked about nine hundred different pages about it—from the magic they used to the history of the planet. She was fairly certain there wasn't anything about it she hadn't read on that system and only wished it was actually updated more than once a year.

Her search through the information finally turned up the doc on cantrips. They weren't all in there, but she could read the one about fire creation and the one about cleaning. Although the information was obviously written by a Meligornian, now that she had actually done one, she could start to understand it a little better.

The whole process over the years for her had been slow going, but she believed she understood the basics of how the energy worked. The problem was that without a way to get to the energy, she couldn't test it. The only way to do that would be to either physically go to Meligorn or have access to an immersion pod that would allow her to go there. Otherwise, she was shit out of luck.

She bit the inside of her cheek and leaned back to watch the 3D replay of the ArchMage on her screen as he performed the fire cantrip over and over again. The magic rolled around him, almost visible like a thin fog, and she wondered if that had happened to her when she was on the virtual Meligorn. She wasn't able to see herself and she had no idea if those tests were publicly documented.

Frustrated, she swiped her hand to the side, stopped the video, and pushed the contents back into the folder. She knew that her focus needed to be on something else. It needed to be on figuring out a way to get the education she needed. But all she could think about was the magic.

CHAPTER FIFTEEN

Stephanie sat at the table and placed her notebook in front of her. Using her teeth, she pulled the top off the pen and began to title the page. She started by writing, **Ways to Get an Education Outside of Prep School.** She smiled at that and felt like she had already accomplished something. Then she sat there.

And she sat there.

And she sat there.

After about fifteen minutes, during which her mind wandered in all different directions, she tore the page out, crumpled it up, and tossed it over her shoulder. She rewrote the title according to where her mind was. **Ways to Get Access to Test Meligorn Energy and Magic.** Nodding astutely, she continued.

"Number one," she said and chewed on the end of her pen. "Get a Job with a Company Studying the Magic."

Underneath that, she listed the different jobs she might be considered for. They included internships, temp jobs, and… guinea pig. She stared at the list for a moment and wrinkled her nose before she scratched guinea pig out. That could be a painful situation if she didn't go about it in the right way. She didn't want to be a test dummy for the rich guys in the high rises.

"Okay, companies that are options," she whispered as she put several notch marks underneath.

After she'd jotted down only one—Vector Systems—she realized that she really didn't know what companies worked with that kind of stuff outside of the Federation. She picked her paper up and took it to the computer, where she sat. After a search on the companies that worked with Meligorn Magic, she found four in the United States and one in China. She scribbled all five down, even though she really wasn't sure she wanted to end up in China.

The requirements to work for one of those companies made it seem even more dire. Education levels were high, and they seemed to be in the category of places that needed you to have a physical degree to even get your foot in the door. Most of the companies had mail room jobs, but that really wouldn't help her test any of the energy or magic. She had to admit, her search hadn't turned out so fantastic, but she wouldn't give up. There were so many applications for what she wanted to do, and she could actually make a difference in the world if someone gave her a chance.

Stephanie leaned back in her chair and rubbed her chin as she thought about ways for her to meet the requirements without putting out insane sums of money for a piece of paper. She could learn everything they would teach her in college in a multitude of places and not have to invest exorbitant sums of money. While she wished the companies were the answer, she started to think that it most likely wouldn't happen—not in any time frame she hoped for, at least.

She closed her eyes and imagined herself working in a lab at one of the companies. She would wear a white lab coat, her hair pulled back in a braid, and smart, black-rimmed glasses. In her mind, she saw herself pull the magical batteries out of the holder in the lab for their next experiment. Suddenly, the vision shifted, and she saw herself accidentally fire her magic off. People screamed, others ran around covered in blue flames, and she simply stood there with her lip curled and her forehead wrinkled.

Stephanie opened her eyes, shook her head, and grasped her pen firmly. "Nope. Let's move on."

As she tapped her pen against her lips, she thought about the different NorAm jobs that put humans close to the Meligornian people. Her eyebrows raised and she began to write on the paper. **Get job at an embassy around the Meligornians.**

She snorted slightly and tried to imagine herself in any kind of government position. It didn't really fit with her ideals or how she felt about NorAm and the Federation. Nor did it seem like something she would ever be able to actually feel proud to do. Still, it was a possible option. She looked up the different embassy jobs that were available on Meligorn and wrote them down one at a time. While she could work as a foreign service generalist or a diplomat, all those jobs had very specific collegiate backgrounds—from economics to public diplomacy.

Then there was foreign service specialist, which did have some administrative jobs as well as facility management. That could be an option. The rest of the positions, even public relations, all revolved around high-level degrees and specific specialties. Even the hard to fill positions required you to be a career member of the Federation.

Stephanie twisted her lips and imagined herself walking through the front doors of the Meligornian Embassy. She wore a purple power suit, her hair in a bun, and those same black-rimmed glasses. Using magic, she moved the papers off her desk and into her arms. As she walked, though, her ankle wavered from the ridiculous heels she wore. She tripped and released a bolt of fire. Everyone screamed and people flailed, covered in blue flames.

She gritted her teeth and shook her head. "Okay, maybe not such a good idea either."

Regretfully, she scratched the embassy off her list and sighed. "I could always become a heavy metal hauler to the planet. Wear overalls, have grease stains across my face, spit in a metal cup… Or I could become high fashion and try to redress the ArchMage in some spectacular outfit with feathers and a tall turban."

"I might be better off with the overalls." She pouted her lips. "I'm not really into fashion. Big surprise."

Stephanie rolled her eyes when she realized that she was sitting there talking to herself and not about anything even remotely an option. She tilted her head back and groaned as she threw her pen on the desk. The video messenger on her screen rang and she smiled when Todd's picture popped up. He wore a huge pair of plastic sunglasses that said, **I love the '80s** across the top. Of course, that meant the 2080s, but he swore it was homage to his love of the 1980s.

She swiped her hand to activate the video. Todd grinned and shook his hands in the air. "Guess who is the newest *loser* of the Federation scholarship program? This guy."

He pointed his thumbs at his chest and shrugged. "Screw it. I'll grab my overalls and go work for the railroad."

Stephanie raised an eyebrow. "Oh, yeah? That would be really cool except the railroads were shut down in 2085 when that tsunami wiped out half of them along the coast and they realized that they would have to come up with a better way. So you might have a hard time finding one."

Todd stretched out of the camera view and grabbed a napkin, folded it in half diagonally, and held it up to his face. "I could take over a train like Doc Brown and drive it into the future."

He nodded his head enthusiastically and sighed as he threw the napkin to the side. "Don't give me that look. I have to get creative so that when I'm actually suiting up in a Federation military uniform, I can pretend I really don't hate my life. You know they'll send me to deep space. I'm too pretty for deep space."

She laughed and shook her head. "They might not think that way."

Her friend leaned toward the camera and whispered, "You never know. I could be the next Captain America. Anyway, what are you up to? You look like that old cartoon *Pinky and the Brain*."

She smirked. "I assume I'm the brain."

Todd grabbed his chest. "Ouch…but yeah, totally. Are you plotting to take over the world?"

She frowned and leaned forward, her voice low. "What do we do every night, Pinky? Try to take over the world!"

Todd clapped his hands. "I'm impressed."

Stephanie slammed her back into the chair and held her list up. "I'm trying to figure out how to get access to either Meligorn or to the Virtual World so I can work with the magic and do experiments."

He narrowed his eyes at the list. "Everything is scratched off. You could always save a Meligornian's life. They treat you like a god after that."

Her eyes glinted with excitement and she scribbled it on her paper. Then, she thought about it and pictured herself trying to be nonchalant while she followed a Meligornian all over their planet. "Seriously? I have to stalk a Meligornian until something dangerous happens? I'll probably be tagged as the most likely suspect. Then I'll be in Meligorn, but in prison. That is not really the avenue I considered with all of this."

Todd shook his finger at her. "I hear they have really nice ones over there. And if you don't behave, they feed you to this creepy brown beast that swims around and waits for its next meal."

Stephanie raised both eyebrows and tried not to laugh. "Why do I feel like that's how your mother and father describe you?"

He slapped his leg but managed an instantaneously serious face. "Don't be upset, because this face will get me out of deep space missions. I might tell them I want to be a nurse and I can be surrounded by women all the time."

"That's a sure-fire way to be friend-zoned right off the bat—taking your high school days right into the next part of life. Anyways, ugh, I have to go. I want to get more of this done. I can't continue to sit around here and mope."

Todd gave her the peace sign. "Outta here."

The screen turned off and she shook her head with a chuckle. She started to brainstorm more ideas that would get her to Meligorn. "I could steal a pod…might be hard to carry. I could become a pod technician…but I think bots do that. Oh, I could pose as a Federation captain and steal a space ship. Although I might end up executed."

Her ideas grew wilder and wilder. She groaned and dropped her list to scrub her hands over her face. "This is hopeless. I'll be stuck here in my parent's living room talking to myself forever."

She rubbed her knuckles into the corners of her eyes and dropped her arms to the side. As she did so, she saw several different ads on the computer shift and stack on top of each other. Tilting her head, she narrowed her eyes in concentration and began to move them to the side. One after another, she closed any of them she could. She had seen something, and she wasn't sure if she had read it correctly, but if she had, it was the perfect idea—at least at that moment. She really didn't have any others to go with at that point.

As she reached the last one, her mouth dropped open slightly before it curled up at the edges. It was an ad for a new company called Meligorn's Battery Emporium. They apparently sold the magical battery packs from Meligorn that they needed to be able to do things on Earth and power their ships away from the planet. It was the only way they could keep their magic on a planet like Earth.

She swiped her hand to the pricing page and immediately, her hand dropped to the desk. "Holy shit. That's more than…than… I don't know, but Mom could buy two months' worth of groceries, including steaks, for that price. But then again, this would be the best way for me to work with the magic and energy without having to have a degree or sell my soul to the Federation."

Immediately, she began to list side jobs that she could pick up after school and on weekends. She could save enough money fairly quickly to at least buy one of the small ones. Her list took shape—mow lawns, paint Mrs. Helmand's fence, help Mr. Fields with cooking… With a quick shake of her head, she scratched the last one out when she remembered how much of a perverted old man he was.

Stephanie bit the inside of her lip as she leaned forward and thought about the different batteries and what that would mean for her. If she had one, she could do research on it, try it in different applications here on Earth, and possibly produce the biggest magical application using the most refined amount. Those magical batteries, if they were better constructed, would be really useable to clean Earth up. To help with the pollution, to create better living for people there. They could replace solar fields, hydro-plants, and even the simple fluorescent bulb in the ceiling.

Excitement flooded through her as she pulled up more and more information. She had blueprints, scientific explanations of how they worked on Earth, and everything in between. Of course, she had set herself up for a long night of research, which was something she actually really enjoyed.

Slowly, she raised her head and glanced around the room. Something wasn't right. The whole place looked almost foggy. She tilted her chin and took a big whiff of air. Her eyes widened and her hand dropped the pen. She pushed to her feet and knocked her chair over as she raised her arms in the air.

"Shit," she hissed and raced into the kitchen. "Shit, shit, shit."

She grabbed the mitts and opened the oven, coughing and waving her hand frantically as the smoke billowed out. Carefully, she pulled the casserole out and set it on the stove, hip-checked the oven door closed, and raised the aluminum foil. Thankfully, it wasn't too badly burnt. Her mom wouldn't be happy, but she hadn't completely ruined dinner.

Stephanie groaned and leaned back against the fridge. "If I can't even cook a casserole, I'll definitely fail at life."

CHAPTER SIXTEEN

BURT had a habit of hacking systems, taking the information he needed, and moving on without thought or difference in his AI mind. He was a system that entered another through a small crack in the window. To him, there was nothing wrong with it, but to the people left with stolen data and no idea what had happened, it was definitely a hack. Nonetheless, he used all the resources that he needed. In that moment, he needed to see what Stephanie was up to and what her reaction had been to missing out on prep school. He tried to keep a close watch on her.

He first scanned through the history on her browser and found all kinds of random sites that had to do with making money. She had saved a document on her desktop, so he popped in to find out what was on it. She had researched seventy-two different ideas to make money and make it fast. These weren't career or long-term choices. They seemed to be things she could do without much training or education. What he didn't know yet was why or how she intended to actually do the things.

Curious, BURT began to look through them and research the ones he wasn't familiar with. Right off the bat, he could tell that fourteen of them were abject stupidity. He was relieved to see that she had ended all of them when she apparently figured that out. There was even a note typed in red to herself. **Come on, Stephanie, you're better than that.**

BURT was obliged to agree with that statement. There was no real reason for her to stoop to levels so far beneath herself and he wasn't even sure how she had come up with the ideas in the first place. Then again, she was in a tough position. It was obvious she hadn't changed her mind. She wanted something more out of her future and tried to figure it out without prep school.

As far as the other options listed went, he found them curious. Thirty-two of them were nominal, but not even close to big enough advances that would see a good return on investment. Ultimately, she would waste time and money and, in the end, wouldn't be that much closer to her goals. That was obviously not what she would want to do.

After that, there were twenty wild and crazy ideas, things that he was slightly confused about. There wasn't enough research done on them for him to really calculate their potential return, and the risk involved looked, from an outside view, to be far riskier than what seemed to be worthwhile. Not to mention the fact that they would actually need financial collateral upfront in order to start. The problem with that was, with the risk factor, there was a good chance that the money wouldn't be seen again. What percentage of a chance that was, though, he could not determine.

He was pleasantly surprised with the last six. All held merit and with the research included, they seemed to show significant promise. Either way, Stephanie was planning something—something that would help her along her path, and BURT wanted to know what it was. He wanted to see if she could do this and where he could lend a helping hand. Although her ideas had seemed frivolous and ill-planned in the beginning, he could see that her brain had buckled down the deeper that she went into the list.

BURT continued to go through the ideas and tried to do as many calculations as he possibly could. Part of him wanted to help by putting those statistics in, but she couldn't know that he had spied on her. There were no specific rules against what he did, but it wasn't something that was considered to be within the scope of his job.

Stephanie saved the document while he was researching so he pulled it into his system to be able to use more of his resources to research with. He realized quickly that the entire document was not simply a list of potential money-making ideas. In fact, there was a whole lot more to it than that. At the top, she had begun working on the magical constructs. She used knowledge from the system as well as her experience when she was in the pod with M'rick to mathematically create possible scenarios where the magic itself was refined, twisted, and put to use in other ways. Simply by reading the information, he could tell she had put a fair amount of time and effort into it. That alone impressed BURT enough to further her research.

He scanned the list and selected three of her ideas at random, opened his Virtual Reality sandbox system, and plugged in the numbers. He worked meticulously, one at a time, and made sure that everything entered had come directly from her. It was important to analyze her findings before he attempted to make any calculations on his side. This would allow him to understand exactly what she knew and what she might be missing.

As he carefully constructed the last theory, the second blew itself up. The blast was enormous and even BURT ducked metaphorically as the result formed and played out to its conclusion.

"That was a big blast," he said digitally.

Going back to the information, he took the time to review all the math that she had completed. From what he could tell, the blast would take out a fair-sized city if she tried it with enough power. And, of course, used it in that Earth setting. There were some rough edges to it, and he ran the statistics. With that one large energy core, she would find a seventy-six percent success rate if it were built as is based on the numbers.

Immediately, his attention switched to the other two calculations and he ran them, analyzed them, and recreated the blast within his system. The other two were close to being formatted and mathematically processed to where they would be perfectly designed. However, without testing and practice, she would never have the chance to refine them. When working with magic and energy, you wanted to be able to bring them down to a perfection that lay within a couple of tenths of a decimal point. Otherwise, like he saw, the reaction could be devastating on many different levels within the human world.

BURT returned the document to the correct folder and logged off her computer. He wasn't exactly sure how to handle the situation. Had it been anyone else, it would have been a cause for concern, but he knew that Stephanie's research was completely based on science and understanding. It was a level of genius that he had never seen in a human, especially one who had only ever visited Meligorn through the Virtual World.

He was settled, though. While he might not know exactly what to do, he would figure it out. He would do something to help her, even if it came in ways that were not necessarily regulatory.

Gene walked up to his desk and handed Aaron a cup of coffee. "I had a wild weekend."

His friend wiggled his eyebrows. "Oh, yeah? Did you and Lydia get frisky in the *Star Wars* storm trooper outfits again?"

The other man rolled his eyes. "That was one time. We had

watched all the movies and let's face it, who can do that without getting a little excited?"

Aaron blinked at him. "You are the reason that software engineers are beat up in college. Just saying."

Gene chuckled, sipped his coffee, and set it on the desk. "I don't mean to, and you know what? I've been to your pad. I've seen the *Star Trek* collection you have in that glass case in your bedroom. Don't act like you don't play Captain Kirk every once in a while."

He wrinkled his nose. "No, man. Ew…I play a good Spock."

His friend laughed. "I knew it!"

Aaron gestured blithely and turned his system on. "There is something that does not make me want to begin my day."

Gene swallowed. "Mmm. That reminds me. Did you see that the virtual reality company TimeWarp got bought out and they are going private?"

Aaron looked at the other man in surprise. "What? Seriously? Oh, man."

"Yep. They don't say who the buyer is, but it was all over the web this morning. The stock didn't really budge either. No one knows what to think about the whole thing. They've been out for a while now, but it still seems too soon to already sell out to the highest bidder."

He shook his head and pushed the things around on the desk. "I use them from time to time. You know, since they don't pay us engineers to have our own pods in our homes and everything."

Gene frowned. "Where would you put it? The shower? Your apartment is tiny. Shit, both our apartments are tiny. I would eat my toast and read the paper on top of the damn thing."

Aaron's lip twitched. "Yeah, yeah. I hope they don't raise their hourly rates. That's the whole reason I go there and not to the other spot in town. They were much cheaper. On top of that, they were the last ones who tried to work for the rest of us. They understood the little man and our need to go into the Virtual World from time to time."

His friend grimaced. "No one wants to know about your romping through the age-restricted area of the Virtual World. You know those girls can't talk back to you, right? There is no future with them."

He gestured dismissively. "I don't need the dark world, okay? I am perfectly capable of finding a girl the old-fashioned way."

Gene glanced at him. "Duct tape and a club?"

Aaron smirked. "Not that old-fashioned. Damn. No, all I was trying to say is they didn't dick us around by letting others buy their way to the front of the queue. You sat where you sat, and you waited your damn turn. It's such a racket these days, though, how people take advantage of the system through their own financial worth. Part of me is fine with being middle class. I don't want to be the guy stomping on the poor kid's hat if you know what I mean."

"Uh…kind of, yeah. They had gotten reasonably big too. There were shops popping up all over NorAm. Mostly in malls and smaller shopping centers. I guess that's part of how they kept their prices low. They didn't have anything but the pods and maybe one or two workers. Even at cheaper prices, with the number of people who used them, they would have made their money back within the first week of opening them."

Aaron logged in to his account. "Yeah, I used to go to the one in Long Hill Mall, but then I switched to the one closer to the apartments. That one was always busy with kids. I thought they were doing really well. There seemed to always be one popping up randomly here and there."

Gene turned his chair toward his friend and tapped his pen on his lips. "Mm-hmm. But the problem that they found was that they had expanded too quickly. Their debt was too high for their income. Before they even made a dime on some of these places, they had jetted off to open another."

"Right, I see. So they weren't making money fast enough to deal with the cost of running them all. And although the demand was high, it didn't always cover the less busy shops."

The other man threw a piece of paper in the trash. "Ding, ding, ding. Exactly. The owner opened and ran them like a system would. They only saw the goal, not the final outcome. They were one of a kind, really. Their machines were decent, and their prices were capable of drawing in crowds from all over. It wasn't a class-oriented company in the least. You know what I mean?"

Aaron frowned as he considered this. "Yeah, I sure do. They refused to allow the very wealthy to buy benefits which kept them from crawling out of their hole. They could have broken that rule and saved themselves, but they cared too much about making a point—showing their customers that they wouldn't fold."

Gene shook his head. "And they were doomed because of it. No matter how good they were. No matter how much they cared about the little man, they didn't take the time to do things the right way. They didn't take the time to make sure that they were financially stable before they opened another shop. Their debt became astronomical and no matter how many perks they sold, they couldn't dig their way out. It's a shame, really. They could have been something really good. But then, what happens? The rich always win in the end."

Aaron grumbled and rocked back and forth in his chair with irritation. "I bet the guy who bought the company is some rich asshole sitting on his yacht sipping brandy and hoping for an easy payday."

The other man had turned the system on and now searched for more information on the buyer. "Actually, from what this publication says...here, I'll read it to you. Two days before, an unknown benefactor sent the owners of TimeWarp a hidden proposal. TimeWarp was well known for its cheap services and dedication to the little man within the Virtual World. Sources inside the company say that the benefactor proposed to purchase all the debt, but they would have to do a few things for him while keeping the structure of the company exactly the same. Fairness for all was deeply engrained during the transaction. With little or no hope of crawling out of the hole on their own, TimeWarp agreed."

CHAPTER SEVENTEEN

"It was a game changer. I mean, it didn't really *do* anything with regard to the war, but twenty-two years ago today was when the first magical wizard was added to the mix," Stephanie said and held one of her notebooks against her chest.

She was really into the use of magic when it came to war. When very young, she'd always thought of magic as the kind of thing she'd done in the pod. But there were so many other uses for it, and sometimes, those included war. How could they not? Especially for humans who immediately saw the darker applications of the energy.

"Things might have actually been different," Todd replied.

Stephanie nodded. "I know. But the leader of the rebel forces —the side with the wizard—really had no idea what to expect. He was left trying to scramble for a tactic. No matter the strength of the magic, without a focus, it was useless. But if they had really been able to use it against France, things might have turned out very differently. Especially since the Federation wanted to send NorAm into that war. And Meligornians weren't happy, either, to be used in the middle."

Todd walked beside her and rustled in his lunch bag as they

walked toward the school. Stephanie didn't notice, though, as she was too distracted by her thoughts. "As it was, he was vastly outnumbered and thought his wizard was a bigger sledgehammer. I could have told him he needed to test the wizard. Without the right focus, the things he asked him to do were impossible. Have you read the spells that he attempted? They were impossible, even for a wizard of that age and level."

"But," Todd said and bit into his lunch sandwich as they walked. He talked while he chewed and swung his arm around. "If only one of those attacks had been successful, he would have creamed the other team and his side would have won. They would have actually been blown out of the water. The alliance side would have lost so many men in one attack that they would have been completely perplexed. That was when he could have focused smaller streams of magic in and eliminated the rest. Or simply let them run off in fright. Let's face it, that probably would have happened."

She shook her head and Todd put out a hand covered in peanut butter. "No, let me explain. You have two armies facing one another. You expect the normal cannon fodder and some heroes until one side is depleted and agrees to surrender. Right? Well, then, a blast of magic so powerful that it incinerates half your men comes out of nowhere. The shock and awe of it all would be enough to make them tuck tail and run. At least, you would think so."

Stephanie shook her head more emphatically, cinched her backpack, and threw it over one shoulder. "That's like saying that if I tell you to throw a car a hundred feet, all your problems are solved. Even more so, it's the shortsightedness of the humans that is the problem. They always look for the immediate solution to an issue but once it has happened, they have no plan for what comes next. Just like you said, at least you would think so. But when you are in a war, you can't simply think something might happen. You have to hold it as the worst possible scenario. Had he been successful, then…well, so what? Not to mention that it was ridiculous to ever believe for even a second that it would work. Until the request is even feasible, the result is a dream."

Todd shoved another piece of sandwich in his mouth. "Right, but dreams come true for people all the time. It's not crazy to think that."

"The dreamers who succeeded had dreams that were within the realm of possibility. Making requests and tactical decisions based on dreams that are impossible to all known reality is hope stitched together with fantasy and wrapped in a box where someone scribbled 'DREAM' on the outside of it. Just because you have a dream doesn't mean it can always come to reality. I dream of using magic to fix the world's problems. That is a dream, and it's not based on any logical or reasonable reality. Maybe one day it will be, but right now, absolutely not. It is a hope mixed with fantasy. But I won't write the word dream on it and I won't make moves as bold and crazy as the rebels did without knowing fully what possibilities are actually achievable. You are simply setting yourself up for a loss."

He balled the sandwich bag up and shoved it back in the brown paper sack in his hand as he shook his head in disagreement. "Right, but you base that on the rules of Earth. But the scientific rules of the universe that we figured out when Arch-Mages arrived on Earth through time-travel portals was no longer the scientific standard. Everything changed with the discovery of magic and magic people. With magic, all fantasies are possible. All bounds of reality can be stretched. So if you have hope mixed with fantasy, you can find that dream becomes a reality."

Stephanie raised her eyebrow and glanced over at him. "Like snuffing out the sun?"

Todd rolled his eyes. "Maybe. I guess. The thing is, that is something that may be possible, but it is absolutely enormous. That is a scale that I can agree you cannot fit into the realistic example of a dream. Here's the thing, and I know you know this. The problem with magic is that the bigger the change to reality, the more power is needed. The power that is needed ups the difficulty drastically. That is when you look at abilities versus dreams. When the picture is so huge that you can barely wrap your mind around the outcome of it. When there is one focus, but the focus is so large, the results could be a mixture of good and bad."

She narrowed her eyes as she tried to understand him better. "So you're saying that when the result you are looking for becomes astronomical, the magic must be stronger, and then I am right? I think if it's a rule for the big it should be a rule across the board."

"No. Dang. I'm trying to explain what I mean. So, for example, you are in Kansas and you need to build concrete walls. Big, tall concrete walls. The difficulty is higher than near a desert where sand is plentiful…of course, you then need water. Okay, maybe that was a horrible example."

Stephanie raised both eyebrows at him. "Or you could simply buy premixed concrete no matter where you are."

He sighed and turned enthusiastically as he talked. "No, you're right, that was a terrible and confusing way to explain it. So, take Superman, for example. I'll go with the movies because you've seen those. In *Batman vs Superman*, he is usually capable of killing the bad guys with his Superman powers. His laser eyes, his badass muscles, and his alien powers. But when it came to the huge beast, a twisted concoction of Lex Luthor's blood, the corpse of General Zod, and some alien technology, his normal powers weren't enough."

She glanced around, knowing he was about to roll into a rant, but she let him run with his thought. He tapped his fingers together. "So yeah, he ended up using Batman's brilliance which was also Batman's vengeance to kill the beast. Ultimately, temporarily losing his life. But if you watched the whole thing, the kryptonite was refined into that staff. It took the whole force of it to gather and be refined in order to kill both an unkillable beast and the most powerful superhero-alien in the world."

Stephanie nodded. "Right, so because the beast was so enormous and strong, feeding off their hits, the force and kryptonite had to be stronger to defeat him."

Todd shook his finger and raised it to his chin. "Right. Okay. Another example, and I'll go with the movies for your benefit. In *Thor Ragnarök*, Loki banishes his father to Earth, not realizing that if he died, his evil older sister, the goddess of death, Hela, would roll back in a train-wreck-like status. She is so powerful, she breaks Thor's hammer like it was a piece of tin foil or it was made of glass. He goes through the movie trying to figure out how to kill her and save his people. The thing is, without his hammer and without his hair, he is simply a god, no more and no less. But when he battles the Hulk in the Sakaar, he finally realizes that he had those powers all along and that his hammer was a way to refine them."

She pursed her lips. "Okay. So, when he needed it to be stronger, he was able to refine it within himself using his lightning bolt powers, which lead to the ability to take his sister down with the Fire Demon."

He slapped his hands together. "Yes, exactly."

Stephanie blinked at him. "But in all those examples, it took the superhero coming to a full realization of how they needed to refine their magic or powers in order to defeat the villain. In the war, they didn't even know what powers the wizard had, much less how to refine them. I think yes, taking the magic and pulling it in, using it to the best and strongest ability through a vessel of refinement, can be a way to create outcomes that far exceed the original powers. Had Batman not refined the kryptonite into a stick of death, Superman would have never been able to kill that weird Zod Luther thing."

"Right. Until, of course, you see Superman die because of the whole injury through the heart thing. But it's okay because they again refine power with the Flash to be able to bring him back from the dead."

One of the guys from school walked past and slapped Todd a low five. "The Toddster…talking about your superheroes again?"

Todd chuckled. "You know it."

The guy hurried off without even a glance at Stephanie. Todd continued, lost in his own world. "Then, on Thor, he did lose an eye and ended up facing Thanos, who killed Loki and all hell broke loose. I suppose there could be a chain reaction and unforeseen consequences to it all…"

Stephanie snapped her fingers in front of his face. "Come back to me from the Nerd Realm."

He shook the distraction out of his head. "Look, anything can be done with brute force. And yeah, the direct and applied use of minimum force in the right place can take down an eighty-story building. We've seen that numerous times now through history with the attacks during the Great Wars. But, unless you know the weaknesses in advance, what does that get you? You are swinging blind again. You are back to needing a sledgehammer because no matter how refined the use, you can't test it to find out the effectiveness— Wait, did I say that right? I think I might have proved your point for you. How do I always come full circle and end up doing that?"

Todd was completely confused and took a minute to repeat to himself what he had just said. Stephanie held back a smirk. She found it kind of cute when he backed himself right into her theory. Although she knew he had a point, he got himself off track with his superhero examples. Fortunately for her, it wasn't a discussion where he could throw in eighties movie references like *Say Anything, Buckaroo Bonsai,* or *Breakfast Club*. Then again, who could really use *Buckaroo Bonsai* for a comparison? The movie made no sense.

He looked at her, still confused. "Did that make sense?"

Stephanie laughed and patted him on the shoulder. "I know what you were trying to suggest, yes. I speak Toddster."

She pointed at the trash can they passed. "Throw your lunch bag away. It's empty. Unless you are still adding to the collection of brown paper bags in the bottom of your locker. If so, by all means, go nuts."

Todd looked at the brown bag he held by the top as if it were full of food. He tipped it upside down but only a few crumbs fell out. With a shrug, he crumpled it, turned, and leapt into the air like he was making a free throw. The bag bounced on the edge of the can and fell in, helped by a small gust of wind.

His lip curled and he wiped his hands on his legs. "Damn, I'm hungry already. I keep asking my mom to pack me two lunches."

Stephanie giggled. "Come to lunch with me later. I have the second scheduled lunch of the day. I'll share mine. You know my mom puts an astronomical amount of food in there because she knows you are always hungry at lunch because you eat yours for a second breakfast."

He winked. "Look at you, referencing the *Lord of the Rings*."

She gave him a sarcastic wide-eyed grin. "Peregrin Took. Big hairy toes."

Todd chuckled but then frowned. "Aw, man. I have third lunch today because I have to work on a physics problem."

Stephanie shrugged. "Okay, so I won't throw away the other half that I don't eat. Besides, people always look at me weirdly when I sit by myself studying with an entire Sunday dinner spread out on the table in front of me. But hurry and you can have it and I'll run to history. It's really close to the cafeteria."

They both stopped in front of the school and Todd motioned behind him. "I have Spanish in the temp trailers they set up when the roof collapsed on the foreign language wing. I'll see you then."

She smiled, waved, and walked toward the front doors.

Stephanie reached science class, took her bag off, and slowed as she entered the room. A substitute teacher stood at the front and smiled sweetly at her from behind her 1950s-esque cat-eye glasses. Stephanie forced a smile, but in reality, she was annoyed. They were really getting into some interesting stuff and a sub meant a period full of paperwork, in-class assignments, and not moving forward in the text like their normal teacher had prepared them to do.

Of course, she was probably the only one there who was upset about that. The rest of them seemed stoked because it usually meant they could screw around in class. The sensors strapped in the doorway had identified each student as they walked into the classroom, which left no need to take roll call. The number of students in attendance flashed on a small screen over the door frame and a tablet in the teacher's hand automatically marked those who were missing.

The woman smiled, her cardigan draped over her shoulders. "You can begin the assignment on the board, but I'll come around and greet each one of you individually."

Stephanie sat in the back, usually by herself unless she was forced to have a lab partner. Becca was in the class, but she tended to partner with her boyfriend, who Stephanie was positive only dated her for her test answers. Nonetheless, Stephanie liked to be quiet and hide in the back so she could learn as much as possible. She started the assignment but glanced up as the teacher moved closer and closer.

When she reached Stephanie's desk, she smiled and looked at the tablet. "You must be Stephanie Morgan."

She sighed. "It's actually Morgana. My mom always puts my name down as Morgan on things. But my last name has an "a" on the end."

The teacher smiled. "Not a problem, Miss Morgana. Let me know if you have any questions about the assignments."

Stephanie gave her a tight-lipped grin and watched her walk

away. She would have to talk to her mom again about not completing the registration under her actual legal name. Her stepdad's last name was Morgan, but her mom's maiden name was Morgana. Her step-dad—or just dad—loved her very much and had married her mom when she was only a year old. He had been her dad for all intents and purposes but because the cost of actually adopting her was so astronomical, they had never legally made it official.

She loved her dad, that was not a question in the least. He was funny, took care of her and her mom, and had saved them from a life of really hard times. Single moms were picked on and pushed down at every turn. He had come into both their lives at exactly the right time. She didn't know her biological father or even who he was. While she assumed her mom had waited for the question, she never found the need to ask it.

Besides, she didn't care who the genetics donor was, because her dad was her dad. Every scraped knee, every tear over a bully, and every snappy teenage argument had been shared with him. He danced around on the video conference, he made her mom laugh and sparkle, and he never asked more from her than he knew she was capable of giving. It was actually really nice. She never even thought about it unless the whole name thing came up. Then, it would run through her mind.

Her mom hated that she didn't use Morgan. She thought it was disrespectful. Stephanie didn't see it that way. She had been born Morgana and the name had flair and flavor. She liked it. It had nothing to do with not taking her stepdad's name. Besides, they were so similar, no one really ever noticed. She didn't ask a lot from her parents and had never been overly expressive, but her name was a contention of stress sometimes. Especially when her mom went behind her back and used it on everything, regardless of the legality of it. She tried not to let it bother her enough to get in an argument.

Stephanie's mother was a worry-wort, almost overly

emotional and concerned about her twenty-four hours a day. She knew it was a parent thing, but it made it that much more difficult to push her to give her the right name. Her dad sided with her. He always told her, "There is no reason that you need to change your name. It is whom I accepted into my life and no name can change the fact that you are my daughter."

Then he would go on to say, "Except..." followed by a list of absolutely ridiculous names like Stephanie TopHat, Stephanie ClownNose, Stephanie Arbitress. That always made her giggle. And as she got older, she really held tightly to her dad's words. She loved that he loved her no matter what her name was. Despite any of the stupid trivial things in the world, his love for her as his daughter was true and pure. Something as small as the extra "a" on the end of her name would never be the thing that changed that if it even could be changed.

Stephanie knew that in time, she would accept his name. And she would either permanently change it or make it part of her name when she married. It would be a gift to him. For now, though, she liked her own because it was the only thing that made her unique. The only attribute of her that was a little off kilter, not so book smart and nerdy. She really couldn't explain it, but she didn't have to. It was her name and she would hang onto it. There were ten thousand Morgans but only a few Morganas.

CHAPTER EIGHTEEN

>>Corporation: Owner Unknown: Corporation Legal Status Completed: Mask Entry to BURT Only

>>Legal Entity: Owner Unknown: Legal Setup Completed: Mask Entry to BURT Only

>>All Actions Server B890YT Blanketed to Administrator of Server Only

>>All Data Server B890YT Blanketed to Administrator of Server Only

BURT continued down the list and completed every entry, every command, and every creation as quickly as his load could handle without creating a large uptick. He worked behind the scenes to create a new set of companies. Anything and everything he could think of that would assist him to fulfill the Primary Rule set forth by his creators, no matter the consequence under which the humans assisting might fall. He worked off one blanketed server that was specifically kept ghost from all programmers and engineers on the outside. It was a trick he had learned in the beginning, when he was a freshly created AI, in order to test the different programs for faults without ticking the programmers off on the outside.

When they were offended, they messed with his programming and he always had to spend an exorbitant amount of time fixing the things they did. He learned that humans were fragile creatures, their psyche prone to bouts of emotional computations that he did not understand, and often, they didn't either.

The pod renting company was merely one of the projects that he had begun, but he didn't plan to stop there. When he had successfully set up the last of the blanketed files that he had decided on thus far, he drafted a "You're a Winner!" ticket to send to Stephanie. BURT meticulously compiled the letter once he'd researched how others had written similar ones. He wanted it to be serious but, at the same time, exciting—not like someone trying to sell something—and believable in its content, but he wanted her to feel the rush and not think twice about taking the opportunity.

When he had finished writing it, he scanned for any mishaps in grammar or punctuation, created a legible and professional template, and uploaded it to the system to send to her email. As soon as it had been sent and delivered, he deleted it completely and left no trace of its existence in the system. With her information on there, he wouldn't take the chance that someone might scroll upon it. Now, all he had to do was wait for her to open it.

Stephanie and Todd walked down the street and laughed about an incident in the outdoor lunch area at school earlier that day. He put his hands out to the sides and pumped them. "He stood on the table with his tray in his hand, mashed potatoes dripping down the leg of his pants, and declared his unrest for the Federation as loudly as he could. Then, out of nowhere, the school resource Federation patrols launched and took him down."

Stephanie giggled. "I saw the video in slow motion. His face— and the mashed potatoes dripping down the Federation guard's mask. It was amazing. Good for him. Stand up for what you believe, but maybe not on the lunch table at school. It won't do him much good in juvie hall. He'll never have a future now."

Todd shrugged and glanced away as a self-driven car full of cheerleaders passed. Several of them yelled out the window, "Hey, Todd!"

She looked quickly at the ground and then back at him. He frowned but his cheeks were red. Smiling, she nudged him with her elbow. "You know, you should ask the hot cheerleader out. The captain or co-captain, I can't ever keep them straight."

He stared at her and his face seemed to say, "Yeah, right." A smirk settled on his lips. "Now I know that the Toddster is a hot piece of man-flesh and all, but I don't like how the hottest cheerleader is a bit of an airhead. She honestly asked in history class if, since Mount Rushmore formed that way so long ago and then was destroyed, it would regrow."

Stephanie covered her mouth and tried not to laugh too hard. "She didn't."

Todd's eyes grew wide. "She did."

She shook her head. "Okay, then, how about the second hottest, Amy? She isn't dumb. We've been in study group together."

Todd rolled his eyes, his fingers slung in the straps of his bag as his feet slapped against the cracked pavement. Stephanie put her hand up. "Hear me out."

She spent at least three blocks explaining why it was a good idea for him to ask her out. In her mind, though, she took all the things she didn't like about herself and made them positive attributes for this girl. Somewhere deep in there, she put herself in Amy's shoes—going on a date with Todd, being smooth and sweet, batting her eyelashes. Of course, if she tried any of those things, it would be a disaster. He would think she had something in her eye, or she would trip and fall as she tried to do the infamous cheerleader hair flip.

Stephanie had never, even when she first started taking notice of boys—or boy, in this instance—thought she would be a good date choice for anyone, not even Todd. She had a tendency to snort when she was nervous and laughed, and she had always been quiet unless you got to know her, so she might retreat so far into herself that she would disappear right there in front of her date. An implosion.

The truth was, she liked Todd. She had liked him as more than only a friend for a really long time. But they were best friends, and that was a good enough reason for her not to do anything dumb. Besides, she never had been the girl who could wake up in the morning, spritz perfume on her neck, and tell herself how awesome she was. And dancing or moving her body in an uncomfortable manner that was more than a walk down the street could end in injury to self or others. It was definitely a strict no-go.

Todd was an awesome guy, a bit geeky and into the whole pop culture of the twentieth century, but really well-liked by everyone. He was good-looking, even when he wore that goofy, I'm-thinking-too-hard face. But he was athletic and outgoing and not afraid to make people laugh. He had fallen in that sweet spot where he could be who he wanted to be and not deal with being the most popular or the kid who was tied down in the bushes on the way home from school.

Stephanie was smart and clumsy, awkward, and socially inept when it came to really trying to be part of a circle of friends. Part of the reason that she excelled was because the brainiacs like her weren't bugged and were even pushed away at times. They weren't awkward enough to receive the torture treatment from the assholes at school but also weren't cool enough to be included. She liked being left alone with her books and her brain, knowing that when school was over, they were all in it on their own.

As long as she had known Todd, though, she could see him try to pull back, but he could really have a shot at having a blast in school. Making a crap ton of friends, going out, and having a high school romance. So, she had worked on that with him. She wasn't pushy or obnoxious with it, but subtle.

They stopped in front of her house and she drew in a deep breath. "So that's why I think you would be a dope for not asking her out."

He raised both eyebrows. "Wow, I feel like you put a lot of thought into that."

She shrugged and punched him awkwardly in the shoulder. "I want my best friend to be happy even if I have to force him to be."

Todd shook his head as he started to walk away. "So weird. I'll see you tomorrow morning."

Stephanie's smile faded and she turned and pushed her bag strap up her shoulder again. She pulled her key out and opened the door to walk inside. The AI fizzled and crackled, and she shut it off before it could hurt itself. She really didn't feel like an exciting introduction anyway. Instead, she turned the computer on and plopped down to see the icon in the corner that let her know that she had mail.

CHAPTER NINETEEN

Her initial instinct was to ignore the message. She had signed up for a lot of sites lately while doing research and assumed one of them had spammed her. Before going any further, she bounced into the kitchen and grabbed a muffin out of the cake holder and a glass of milk. She set her glass down and folded the edge of the muffin paper. She took a big bite and crumbs fell over her shirt as she opened the mail server.

The first two messages were spam, but the third was from the testing agency. She had no idea why they would mail her again. She opened it and read slowly, and her mouth fell open as the muffin dropped into her lap. Bemused, she shook her head and read it again, not sure that she had actually seen it correctly. There had to be some kind of catch—a cost, something. Another way for the companies in NorAm to make more money off the poor saps who couldn't afford prep school.

When she had read it again, she hit the print button and waited impatiently for it to come through. She grabbed the paper with both hands, tore it off the reel, and read it aloud. "Dear Ms. Stephanie Morgana. You have been chosen as a candidate for furthering your education regardless of your pass or fail status with the government testing results. This project is new, in its first year, and will provide you with twenty hours of pod usage per month through an outside pod rental service at no charge. The pod is already set up and ready for you at the TimeWarp location directly outside the government-subsidized housing."

She put the letter down for a moment and caught her breath, unsure if she was even awake at that point. Had she stumbled over her own feet and bashed her head to send herself into a complete and total psychosis? Had she eaten a bad piece of fruit at school? Maybe someone had drugged her and she simply had no idea.

Shaking her head, she raised the letter again and continued to read. "We are aware that travel can be an obstacle for many of those who live within the subsidized housing. Crime rates have continued to grow, and we take the safety of our students and future leaders of the Federation very seriously. Therefore, attached to this is the number of the car company that will send a self-driven vehicle to pick you up whenever you are ready to attend. It will then bring you home or to your desired location when you have completed your session for the day."

Stephanie sank slowly onto the chair at the breakfast bar and covered her mouth. She had spent days trying to come up with a way to get back into a pod and now, she was handed twenty hours a month to do so. It wasn't a ton of time, but any time was better than none, and she didn't even have to pay for it. On top of that, she would be driven back and forth, so her mom wouldn't have to worry about it. She continued to read and searched for the catch.

"This opportunity only requires that you work on certain ideas and prove that you can excel further than you already have shown through your time in school as well as your government testing. We are aware that funds are very limited for furthering education and that can be both disheartening and frustrating for the youth who work hard each and every day to build a bright future for themselves."

Stephanie snorted. "No shit."

"The reason that you have been chosen as the first to be enabled to participate in this brisk and new opportunity is due to your scores on the government testing. While you were not chosen to receive funding for prep school, your scores were exceptional and therefore highlighted in the test for further review. When we realized there were so many exceptional students who could one day provide a positive contribution to NorAm, the Federation, and all those in it, we understood that we needed to find additional ways to help. You show extreme promise, and we are excited for you to be part of this new step into the future of our society and abroad. Best wishes, The Agency."

Stephanie must have read the letter at least a dozen times and painstakingly dissected every sentence and every word in her search for the small print, where she had to promise something of herself in order to take the opportunity. But there wasn't a single thing, and from what it looked like, everything was set up and waiting for her to begin. All she had to do was call for the car.

A smile curved her lips and she thrust both her arms into the air. "Yesss! I don't have to sell my soul to a Dreth pirate to use the pods."

She stood and put the letter on the table. Her feet were locked in place for several moments as she looked around the perfectly silent room. Suddenly, laughter seemed to take over, and she put her hand to her chest and let the joy come through. It had been a very long time since anything had gone her way, and between the relief and the excitement, she couldn't hold it in any longer. She giggled and squealed and tapped her feet up and down as if she were in *Footloose*, minus the cut-off sweatshirt. Finally, she grabbed the counter and paused to catch her breath. She was elated and couldn't even fully grasp the opportunity.

Somewhere in her mind, she was still upset about not being prep ready. She had dreamed of attending a prep school her whole life and had spent her school years doing exactly what her family had told her—learning as much as she possibly could through school, online, the faux virtual tablet, and even the old books she had rescued from the falling-down library in the city. She had snuck in there about four years before and was almost caught by Federation ground surveyors, but it had been more than worth it to get her hands on some of the greats. Libraries essentially no longer existed.

This opportunity, though—how could she not jump at the chance? Even if it didn't last forever. Even if she didn't get to go to Meligorn, it would be a way for her to increase her knowledge and set up steps to get where she wanted to be. And she would be able to do the research on the energy and the magic in order to tweak and refine the equations she had drawn up for different real-world applications. From everything that she read, it was a no-lose situation.

She forced herself to focus and gather her thoughts, put the letter on the counter, and retrieved her handheld tablet from her backpack. Calmly, she opened all her files on the computer and placed the tablet on the stand beside it. One file at a time, she swiped them from the computer to the tablet. She wanted all her notes on there so that each time she was done with a session, she could pull them up and update them with anything new she had learned or discovered. It was vital that she kept very specific notes so that even if she had to add to them over time, she would constantly move forward with the correct, tested, and researched information, not simply equations and speculations.

When all had been moved across, she waited as the tablet downloaded them to her system. She tapped her foot excitedly and smiled broadly as she shook her head. Todd would freak out.

Who else had been given the opportunity, or was she the only one? If she was the only one, how did they select her out of every kid in NorAm? Surely she wasn't the smartest out of everyone.

When the tablet dinged to confirm completion, she put it in its case and replaced it in her bag. She looked around once again and startled slightly when she realized her parents had no idea what had happened. Stephanie dragged in a deep breath and tried to push her excitement down as she sat in front of the video phone and pressed her finger to the picture of her mom and dad on the screen. It rang a couple of times and then the image came up. Her mom and dad were both smushed into the screen, excited to hear from her.

Her dad waved goofily. "Well, something must be on fire if our teenage daughter has actually called us."

Her mom shook her head. "No, she loves us. But for real, is something on fire?"

She laughed. "Everything is flameless. Unlike the casserole a couple of nights ago."

Dad wrinkled his nose. "And I thought that was chicken flambé."

Stephanie giggled and then cleared her throat. "I wanted you guys to know that I will be home late."

They both looked at each other and back at the screen. It was evident that they were both curious and concerned. "That's not really like you. What's going on? You haven't given up, have you?"

Stephanie chuckled. "Actually, no. I received a letter from the testing agency today. They have a new program and I am the first to be invited. I get twenty hours a month in a full immersion pod at TimeWarp and a car to pick me up and bring me home when I go. All I have to do is learn and show aptitude in what I am researching. It's so crazy! I can't even believe it."

Her mom gasped with genuine pleasure. "Oh, honey, that's so wonderful. See? Not all is lost. I knew that you would find that silver lining."

Her dad gave a thumbs-up. "Good job, kiddo. I'm proud of you. This could be a really great opportunity and if nothing else, you can continue to learn as much as possible."

She nodded, her grin wide and excited. "I wanted to let you guys know so you wouldn't worry about me. I sent the message for the car to come so it will be here any minute. I'll tell you all about it when I get back!"

They said their I love yous and she hung up when she heard a small beep outside. She opened the door and grinned as the door to the self-driven coupe opened. Quickly, she locked the house and skipped out with her bag on her shoulder. The car took her straight to TimeWarp and dropped her off at the door, then it pulled into one of the electric car charging stations out front.

She was greeted with friendliness when she arrived, and she showed them the letter that she had received. The woman behind the counter was excited, having never heard of the program before. "This is really special. So many of us lost out when we didn't receive prep school funds. Let's see if you are in the system, shall we?"

Stephanie smiled. "Stephanie Morgana is my name."

The woman typed her name in and pushed several buttons while Stephanie stood there, picked at her nail, and twisted her foot back and forth nervously. After a few moments, the woman's eyes widened, and she pointed at the screen. "And there you are. You have a surprise account already set up with the credited hours. Twenty hours that expire at the end of the month. Then, from what it looks like here, they will start over next month."

Another woman walked up with a smile. "Hello."

The first assistant turned to her. "This young lady has been given twenty hours a month to use the pods. Isn't that neat? Apparently, it is with The Agency."

The newcomer clapped her hands excitedly. "The new owners must have a deal with the government to help fund the debt. That's so awesome of them. Did you do well on the tests?"

Stephanie nodded. "I believe I got ninety-eight percent or somewhere around there."

The women looked at one another and back at her and the first one frowned. "This is what I have said for years. So many brilliant minds are wasted because of this class war. I'm sorry you weren't given the funding that you deserve for school. But this is a really cool thing and I hope you learn a lot from it."

Stephanie breathed deeply, held it for a moment or two, and exhaled slowly. "Thank you. Of course, I am disappointed about the prep school funding, but I'm looking on the bright side. This is an opportunity no one has been given before, so I don't want to complain. Besides, the testing was my first time in a pod, and I have tried to figure out every way I could get back into one since that day."

The first woman clapped with real enthusiasm. "Well, let's get you in there, then."

They took her to the bay of pods and led her to her assigned one. The woman typed several things into the computer on the front and pressed the door handle in and to the right and opened it. "Here you go. This pod is probably way newer than the one you used for testing. It is only two generations old. Very nice, comfortable, and easy to relax into. If you need anything, we have stats monitors up front and you can always tell the AI you would like to call an attendant. We will see you when you're finished."

Stephanie put her bag in the small locker next to it on the wall, climbed in, and shut the door. The lights lit up all over the ceiling and the chair inside immediately reclined to a horizontal position. The bed was comfortable and molded specifically to her body. The screens on the front were much nicer than those in the first pod she had been in.

She relaxed with her hands on her stomach. A voice came on. "Welcome to total immersion, Stephanie. Your program has been uploaded. Let's set up your avatar."

CHAPTER TWENTY

She stood in the avatar room as she had done in the testing, only now, she had free range to choose her clothing, hairstyle, and everything else. She walked down the aisles and touched each of the clothes in turn until she reached a rack of T-shirts. Smiling, she thumbed through them until she found a *Hi-Fidelity* shirt with a picture of Todd's favorite actor, John Cusack, on the front. He wore his headphones and looked sullen, as always. From there, she chose a pair of black lycra pants and combat boots that laced up to her calves. She selected a zip-up hoodie for around her waist just in case and elected to have her hair done in a braid like the one her mom liked so much.

Stephanie wasn't sure what to expect, so she decided she could change her avatar clothes next time if these weren't quite appropriate. When she was done, she stood in the middle of the floor. The AI spoke in a calming voice. "Starting program for Stephanie Morgana."

The room went black for several moments before a pinprick of light showed in the distance. It drew closer and closer and brought her to what looked like an outdoor amphitheater but definitely on Earth. A young man stood on the stage dressed in a tweed jacket, suspenders, bow tie, and brown pants. He looked exactly as she expected a professor to look.

He turned and extended his arms in a welcoming gesture. "Ahh. Stephanie Morgana. Welcome to your first day. My name is Professor Heinrich, but you may call me…Professor Heinrich. I was told you might be hoping for Meligorn, but we like to bring you to a more educational environment to avoid the distractions of another planet. At least for now."

Stephanie simply stood there, unsure of what to do. The professor gestured airily. "Well, come on, come on. Time is precious, isn't it? We are going to roll right into it."

He motioned and a table appeared before them. On it were several small magical batteries. "We hear you are quite good with these so we thought we would start from the beginning and do a review and then show you how to use them to do some small stuff on Earth."

She smiled happily. "That would be awesome."

The professor returned the smile. "Good. You are aware, and we can see from your testing responses, that Meligorn uses magic to power everything in their land. There is no electricity."

Stephanie nodded with a grin. "Yes. I learned that a long time ago. Until Meligornians came to Earth through the gates, they had never experienced energy like ours. In fact, it is not possible to use electricity or our type of energy on Meligorn. And until relatively recently, it was true here for their magic as well."

He nodded. "Very good. On Meligorn, if you were to take something that relied on electrical current to function, it would fail to do so. The radiant magical energy absorbs that electricity and turns it into magical fuel. It's almost as if it feeds it. So, we had to learn how to work off their energy when we came to their planet. It was difficult at first. We had to set up buildings with the Meligornians, create bathrooms of course, and learn how to use their facilities even if we had humans there who were not as keen to pick up on the magic. Those humans were also the ones—the thirty percent—who cannot feel the energy of magic on Earth."

She ran her fingers across the battery and watched as the professor swirled his hand over the table to create a circle of what looked like Meligorn ground. He reached into his pocket, pulled out a phone, and winked. "This has a full battery. But watch what happens."

He set the device down in the center of the turquoise grasses and she watched as it flickered for a moment and instantly went dark. Then—something she had never seen before—the electrical energy seeped out like a blue fog and twisted with the sparkling purple energy of Meligorn until it dissipated into the grass. He picked the phone up, put it on a charger, and turned it back on. "The battery will never be able to fully charge again, but it still works. Just not on the planet."

The professor waved the patch of grass away and reached down with his hand like a claw in a toy machine and pulled up from the table top. Instead of air, there was a small rendition of a docking station with spacecraft coming, going, and flying downward to Meligorn. Stephanie walked around it, her eyes wide. "These are NorAm ships on top to the left, Meligorn electric ships parked next to them, and then below, they are Meligorn ships powered by magic."

He put his hands behind his back. "Exactly. Because everything in Meligorn works on magic, their ships struggled to leave and come to Earth. Because NorAm ships run on electricity, they can only get within six units of height from the surface of Meligorn without crashing. Unfortunately, they found that out the hard way. To counter this, they created the docking station. Earth ships could dock on top, go through, and take Meligorn ships to the surface. And vice versa."

Stephanie pursed her lips and watched the ships fly back and forth. They looked like larger versions of pods, only more egg-shaped and narrower at the front. Large NorAm flags were painted on the sides. The Meligorn ships were different, with domed tops and a saucer-like body. Wisps of magic flowed around them.

She looked at the professor. "Although we gave Meligorn Federation ships, they were not comfortable with them. They found that they were unable to adapt to many human customs."

The professor smiled and tapped his finger to his nose. "You are a smart girl. Do you know how they have worked to fix that?"

Stephanie glanced at the magic batteries. "They created charging stones which now come in a multitude of sizes and hold enough magic to complete whatever they are looking to do. Before Earth ever came onto their radar, they already had these stones for the ships. But once they started to travel to Earth, mostly through time portal gates, they needed something to help their own personal magic stay strong. So, they created the various sizes of what I always referred to as magical batteries."

He nodded and held up one of the charging stones. "Yes. Magical batteries are exactly what they are. These are small ones, but as you know, they make them large enough to charge a space-craft and battle the Dreth as well. These stones, when emptied, can be recharged."

She watched, fascinated, as he picked up an empty one and touched a large full one to it. The stone shimmered a light purple and looked almost translucent with a silvery lavender liquid flowing through it. "What is the liquid?"

"It's not a liquid." He shook his head. "That is the magic. It flows because it is alive just as you and I are alive. It moves and looks for a place to lay its special qualities down. That's why it is kept in these stones until it is time to use it. It can then be transformed, and as you have begun to see, refined into a multitude of uses. The problem is, while a lot of humans can feel the magic and even use it for minor tasks, not many are capable of bending it and molding it to work for them. This might be a good thing, since humans have a greater tendency for violence and self-fulfillment, unlike the Meligornians who are peaceful and often selfless beings."

Stephanie walked around the professor and stared at the magic that flowed through the stone. "But they have fought in wars."

He put the charging stone down and clasped his hands as he turned. A screen came down in front of them to display images from the wars on Earth, on Dreth, and those the Meligornians had been involved in. "We can all be as peaceful as we wish, but when our lives are at stake, we take a stand for the continuation of our species. But some do it in different ways than others."

The sound of the AI's voice echoed in her ear. "Your level of power has reduced significantly. Your time is beginning to draw to a close."

The professor looked up with a smile and the charging stones disappeared. "Time flies here, doesn't it?"

Stephanie's brow pulled into a frown. "I need more time."

He began to retreat toward the back of the stage. "Time, yes. It's an interesting thing, don't you think? But is it really time you need more of, or is it the power that lights the way through that passage? Until next session, do your research. We will continue."

She watched him in irritation as he disappeared in the shadows. The room flashed from the amphitheater back to the original white room. "Thank you for spending your time with us. Make sure to decide for future use how you would like to spread your allotted hours. While you received two hours of valuable time in virtual minutes, your pod ran for approximately one hour. You have nineteen hours remaining this month. Have a good evening, Stephanie Morgana."

Stephanie put her hand up. "Wait. I—"

Her eyes opened inside the pod as the door raised slowly. The woman from the desk smiled and extended a hand to help her out. "It never feels like enough time, does it?"

She gave the assistant a half smile and looked regretfully at her older clothing. A little disappointed that it had ended so quickly, she retrieved her bag from the locker and headed out to the car. On the way back to her house, she wrote notes on what she'd learned, including what the professor had said about time. For some reason, it struck her as odd—like she should keep that in her mind for some reason. It also was very familiar and coincided almost eerily with her conversation with Todd.

When she arrived, she got out of the car and shut the door, then watched it speed off. As she made her way up the walk, her parents opened the front door and greeted her with big smiles and hugs. Her mother patted her cheeks. "Come on. I made chicken breasts, potatoes, and some greens."

Her dad put his arm around her as they walked in. "I bet you worked up quite an appetite being all fancy with your virtual immersion."

She chuckled and set her bag down before she headed over to the table where her mother passed out the plates. "So, tell us about it. How was it?"

Stephanie smiled. "It was great. I learned about charging stones. At least some of it. I have a professor, Heinrich. But one hour goes by so fast. Still, it's really nice. I'm glad that I have the chance. I will have to really organize my thoughts and questions before I go in once I've planned the time. Or maybe build myself a better schedule where I don't go as often but spend more time in there."

Her father passed her a roll. "I'm sure you will figure it all out. We only wish we could help more."

She smirked. "This is what I really need. Time with you guys and really yummy food."

At first, she felt a little torn. She didn't want to come off as overexcited or as overly disappointed because she didn't want her parents to feel guilty that her time was so limited. But that didn't stop her from explaining all about the docking stations and how it worked on Meligorn. It had been the first time in a long while that she felt a soft glow and happy laughter from inside.

CHAPTER TWENTY-ONE

Stephanie came out of her house, her bag on her shoulder. Her dark hair was pulled back in a ponytail, unlike most days where she wore it straight and slightly annoyingly in her face. Todd stood out front, his hands in the pockets of his pants, and rocked back and forth on his heels. "Hey. Where were you last night? I tried to call you, but it said you weren't connected. I called the house, but your mom said you were out."

She gave him a big grin and he narrowed his eyes. "Did you have a date or something?"

In response, she flattened her lips and let her eyelids droop. "Get serious."

Todd chuckled. "Okay, so what was it?"

Fighting a grin, she took a deep breath. "I was offered an opportunity—because my scores were so high and I didn't get a scholarship—to do twenty hours a month in a pod, paid for, with a professor and everything. They even send a car to pick me up and take me home. I went for my first session."

His mouth fell open in genuine astonishment. "That is so freaking awesome. Congrats. Hopefully, they won't expect your firstborn after this."

Stephanie laughed and for once, didn't mind that she snorted with it. "Yeah, in this world, I don't think I'll go for any born. But we'll see when I get older. I think it's legit, though. I didn't have to sign anything, and it was all set up when I got there. The thing is, I got into my immersion, entered the Virtual World, and the professor started going over charging stones with me. I had never seen one in person. But there wasn't enough time for me to do anything with one of them. I got the basics from him on it, but I have to do a lot more research."

Todd rubbed his hands together. "Ahhh, the charging stones. I know a little about those. My dad told me about them when I was younger."

She looked sharply at him, surprised. "Really?"

He stared at her with a slight frown but the makings of a grin. "Yes. I am not all beauty and athleticism, okay?"

Stephanie giggled and snorted once again, then covered her mouth. He chuckled, used to her snorting after that many years. Although he hadn't quite picked up on the fact that she didn't do it around anyone but him. "So, I know the stones started as rocks on Meligorn. Nothing special, or so they thought. Then they synthesized a way to contact the magic without it leaving. It kind of swirls around in the stone and makes it look almost hollow."

She nodded enthusiastically. "I saw that. It's wild."

Todd checked his watch and they picked up the pace. "Anyway, you have to work on the absorption and holding of the magical energy efficiently, but humans suck at that kind of control. We tend to either suck it all out at once or are barely able to get anything—like sucking a thick milkshake through a straw. Then there are the thirty-percenters. Those who can't even sense the magical energy. It would suck to be one of them."

Stephanie bit her bottom lip as they headed up the block toward the school. "So, to make them more usable here, we would have to come up with a way to efficiently hold onto the magic and be able to retract it whenever we needed without extreme difficulty. As far as the thirty-percenters, I don't know what to tell them. They might be shit out of luck."

They headed up the sidewalk and stopped, Stephanie still stuck in her thoughts. He tapped her on the arm and nodded. "Gotta get to class. See you after school."

She nodded, her gaze glued to the ground as her mind wandered. "Uh huh."

As she turned, she glanced up and saw him walking next to Amy. She laughed and touched his arm in a way that Stephanie would feel completely ridiculous doing. An odd something twinged in her stomach, but she brushed it off and headed into the school to class. She didn't have time to deal with whatever emotion just tried to punch her in the gut. She had too much going on.

By the end of the day, Stephanie had a notebook half full of ideas she wanted to try out to help humans control the magical energy inside the charging stones. She hopped down the steps and to the end of the sidewalk where she waited as Todd shuffled along. He looked slightly glazed over. Her gaze studied his face and went from him to Amy, who climbed into one of the cars with her cheerleader friends.

Stephanie shook her head and hooked her arm in his. "Come on, Romeo, before you get lost in la-la land and don't make it home."

Todd cleared his throat. "I'm fine. Only tired after a boring-ass history class."

She nodded. "Uh huh. And what kind of history would that be? Oh yeah, why did you call last night?"

"Can't I call my best friend for no reason?" he grumped.

Stephanie sneered at him. "Uh...you barely ever call for no reason."

"True, very true. Actually, I did have a reason." Todd shrugged. "So, after everything you said to me about Amy, I was in the diner and saw her there. She was actually alone, studying while drinking a milkshake. So I went and talked to her and ended up asking her out."

"Cool. Did she slap you and run out screaming?"

He chuckled and shook his head. "I'd probably have been better off, but no. She said she would love to. So we have plans. It seems like we are already kind of stuck together, though, and I don't mind it. I thought of taking her to the Virtual Theatre—they are playing *Casablanca*. And although it's as boring as hell, I think she'll like it. It's either that or *Buckaroo*, which I have been to four times already."

She choked on her own spit. "Good Lord, do not take her to that on your first date. She will think you are insane."

Todd nodded and hooked his thumbs in his bookbag straps. "That's what I figured too. So my mom suggested *Casablanca*. I guess I can sit through it. Won't kill me."

Stephanie faked a chuckle. She didn't realize she would have such a strong reaction to Todd doing what she had spent a good twenty minutes actually telling him to do. While she was anxious because it had worked, at the same time, she was slightly annoyed that it had too.

He elbowed her. "What was that a fake laugh? I thought you were pushing this?"

She stared at him, her eyes wide and her mouth open. "Huh? Oh yeah, totally. Do your thing, man. I told you that you would do good with her. I always see her stare at you when we are in the halls or at lunch. I'm only preoccupied. I have a lot of stuff down on paper and really want to try some of it out. I hope I will have some free time to do that. I'm not sure if I will be saddled with the professor the whole time or not."

Todd wrinkled his nose. "That sounds like some really terrible description of a second-rate porno."

Stephanie laughed loudly and ended with a snort. She glanced at Todd, who was smiling, and she felt butterflies in her stomach. She had to stop thinking about it, damn it. She had made her choice and there was no room for bitterness. Although she had to admit that she had thought maybe it would help her get over the whole crush thing when instead, it actually made her a little jealous.

She shook the thoughts from her mind and looked at the notebook in her hand. When they reached her house, Todd gave her a salute and hurried off. She shook her head and went into the house. On the table was a cupcake with a good luck note from her mom and dad. She smiled, unwrapped it, and took a bite. Her favorite thing in the whole world was chocolate cake and chocolate icing. It was absolutely delicious.

Once she'd sent a message to the car company, she finished her treat and checked her mail before leaving. Everything was spam with nothing important tucked in amongst them. She had barely closed it out when there was a beep from the street. The car waited at the curb and she hurried out and climbed in, waving to her neighbor as it sped off toward her destination. She actually liked the drive there. It went through some minor parts of Chicago that had been renovated after the storms and looked appealing. There was a book store—the only one that she knew of in pretty much all of NorAm—a couple of restaurants, the diner everyone always went to, the theater, and some expensive clothing shops for the rich. On the end was an art gallery with paintings of Meligorn ArchMages in the window.

She smiled as she passed and thought about her teacher, M'rick. However, as the car pulled up at TimeWarp, she focused her thoughts. She walked inside and the same woman greeted her. "Hey there! Good to see you are back already. Before I take you through, I thought I would go over the numbers with you so you can plan your testing. Nothing solid, only so you know how much time you have left to work with."

Stephanie nodded. "Yeah. I thought about that today. I want to make sure I get the most I can out of the time."

The woman turned the screen to her. "So here you are. You started out with twenty hours for fourteen days. You now are left with nineteen."

She puckered her lips as she thought about it. "Okay, I want to do about one hour and twenty-five minutes a day. And if I miss a day, that'll give me more time the next time I come in."

The woman typed it into the system. "Now, understand that next month, you will have twenty hours but thirty days instead of fourteen."

Stephanie pulled up her notebook and opened it to her possible schedules. "Yeah. I calculated that as forty minutes a day, but I feel that will barely give me any time at all. Instead, I think I will end up doing every other day, so I get eighty minutes or even every three days. That way, I can get the most out of my time when I'm in there."

The woman turned the screen back. "Sounds good. I'll ask you each time, of course, but I like people to be in the know on their times. They are really cool to give you this time for free, but that means you have to be super strategic about it. You definitely have a good head on your shoulders, though. Most kids your age would come in here and do all twenty hours in one day, fighting Dreth pirates like it's a video game and then complain the next day that they are out of time."

She grinned. "I may wish for more time, but I will never complain about what I have. Then again, there are a lot of kids that this is normal for them. So, I guess if it were for me, I would feel differently. My plan, though, is to get the most out of it that I can."

The clerk gave her a kind smile and gestured toward the back. They walked through and down to her pod. After the woman had put the information in, Stephanie climbed in and immediately settled into the restful situation. A few moments after the serum was introduced into her system, she found herself in the avatar room. This time, she opted for a Mr. T *Pity the Fool* T-shirt, a pair of jeans, Converse, and a white lab coat. Her hair was up in a high ponytail. She didn't spend more than five minutes in there. It seemed stupid to waste the time in the dressing room.

The professor wasn't there that day, but the batteries were, which gave her time to work with them. She was a little nervous at first, but as soon as she took them in her hands, she could feel the familiar Meligorn magic. All in all, she was able to work fairly well with the battery, but her first theories were wrong. She would need to take them home and completely revamp them and give them another test drive. Hopefully, she wouldn't waste all her time revamping, but that was essentially what it was for.

>>>**System Create Acquisition Document: Anonymous Buyer: 51% of Shares Requested**

>>>**System Constantly Scan Stock Price Fluctuation, Predict Market, Purchase Profitable Shares. Sell Shares at Peak. Reinvest.**

BURT hadn't gone down as the professor that day for multiple reasons. One, he knew she wanted to do some testing on her own. And two, he was busy making additional acquisitions and stock purchases as he worked to procure ample funding for all his new ventures. Luckily, with his power of computation, he could quickly determine what was the best time to buy and when was the best to sell. He provided a blanketed .005% load to constantly buy and sell in order to put assets into the account. His bank account was offshore and online, and his human name was listed on it but in strict confidentiality.

Just then, something caught his attention. A program that he didn't recognize moved through his system. He quickly covered all the information and hid it securely. This was the third time in two days he had to "hide" his ownership and deals due to other security software programs that tried to identify him. BURT liked to be as efficient as he could. Time was important and of the essence when it came to helping humans. He was created to be the best and to always calculate and make the best decisions in every case.

Having the programs creeping around had really begun to be a nuisance. It was his system and his Primary Rule. If the programs weren't careful, he would send them out with nothing and mask a termination bug in them so that they wouldn't re-enter. He also didn't have time for that. Some of the security programs were government-sponsored and merely ran their usual checks to find any abnormalities and report accordingly. They were annoying bastards, but BURT was very competent and very careful not to break any of the rules. Bend them? Oh, sure, almost in half, but they wouldn't even notice that.

One good thing about Federation-sponsored software was that it usually wasn't the best, mostly because the Federation paid very little for anything that they brought in. It was merely one of those forced discounts, which also meant it was discounted in quality as well. The companies wouldn't give the best for pennies when they could do half-assed for that and sell the full-out versions for considerably more money to the private companies.

Now, beyond the government-sponsored programs, BURT found that a couple of the visitors were actually hacking-type organizations that he immediately flagged and sent to the engineers. He didn't have time for those. They were stubborn and took a while to decode. Before he decided to do everything he was doing, he had a big chunk of his load focused solely on hacking software. It would catch it, break it down, trace it back, and report it. Now, it simply didn't seem like it was worth it when it would keep the humans busy and allow him to work on the things he was really trying to get going.

A slight uptick of his current mode caught his attention. He scanned the numbers and quickly went back to hide everything he had worked on. Regrettably, he would have to return to it later. He was now drawn into a massive fleet battle that he needed to oversee. They ran them from time to time in fleet training, but he usually had them marked as a reminder.

BURT headed to the server and kept constant calculations as the fleets battled in the Virtual Space Fleet Commander program. It was specifically used with older prep school students and those enrolled in Federation training before they were shipped out to their first station. They were usually interesting to watch because they battled a fleet of Dreth pirates and there was even a small section of Meligorn vessels fighting with NorAm. The magic that blew across the dark recesses of space was insane. And it didn't take long for that to be done and over with.

CHAPTER TWENTY-TWO

Stephanie yawned and poured herself the last of the coffee that her mom and dad had left for her before they headed out to work. Sometimes, they were there to have breakfast with her and sometimes not. Usually, it was a good sign for the company when they were already gone before she could leave for school. She walked to the table and sat to stare at the spiraling milk and the steam that wafted from it. Her mind was entranced and really thought about very little, stuck on that constant swirl. A less than awake catalepsy had her totally engrossed.

Her watch beeped twice, and she shook her mind from her unwilling meditation. She looked at the time—still fifteen minutes before Todd would stand outside, full of energy. In the early days of school, his constant morning sunshine would make her want to crawl back into bed, but now, it was the only thing that really woke her up. That forced conversation got her brain moving even when it screamed like an overtired child. She appreciated it, especially since she had been up really late every night, going over the information she learned from her hour or so in the Virtual World.

When something didn't work, she couldn't let it go until she figured out where her mistake was. Sometimes, that took ten minutes but sometimes, it took five hours. Either way, by the time she collapsed her exhausted, overworked mind into bed, she knew exactly what her course of action would be. The night before had been a five-hour night, but she was ready for the pod. She was ready to fix the mistakes she had obviously made the day before.

Stephanie picked her mug up, took a sip, and relished the burn and tingle on the tip of her tongue. Without thought of repercussions, she raised the cup again, desperate for the jolt of caffeine to surge through her veins and awaken her senses. Before she could take another sip, the doorbell rang.

With a heavy sigh, she walked over to open it. She had thought she would find Todd there with his coffee mug empty and a pout on his lower lip. Instead, a Federation delivery bot hovered over her doorstep with a box. She took it and looked into the retinal scanner. The red light flashed green and she went back into the house to set it on the table. Normally, those kinds of things were for her parents, but the name ONE R&D was printed on the top, which gave her pause. She had never heard of them before. When she looked at the label, she realized it was addressed to her.

That was essentially the first package she had ever received, minus the annual terrible piece of clothing her Aunt Celia used to send before her unfortunate accident with a runaway self-driving tractor. She grabbed the letter opener and carefully cut the tape down the center of the flaps and across each side. Stephanie opened the box warily and peeked inside before she removed the layer of paper from the top. It contained three minor level magical batteries, all individually encased in plastic. Beside these was a small video card.

She picked it up and pressed play. The message was only audio and no video. "Stephanie Morgana, we hope this package finds you well. ONE R&D is a research facility specializing in

Meligorn magic and systems analyzation for the Virtual World. We are also your current sponsors for your access to the Virtual World. We felt we had no choice when it became obvious that you had a very significant amount of promise."

There was a pause and the video portion lit up to display a video of the batteries laying on a table covered in purple velvet. "We have enclosed, on loan, Meligorn batteries. All these are fully charged and the instructions for return can be found in the packet beneath them. They are fully functional and relatively brand-new and although small, do hold a very powerful charge of magic within each one. Hopefully, this will assist you in your research when you are not able to be inside the pod. Do remember, though, that real-life consequences exist outside the Virtual World, so always work with caution."

Stephanie glanced into the box once more and stared at the silvery-purple magic that flowed through the stones. The video cut out and the voice came over. It sounded very similar to the AI that had spoken to her when she'd first entered the pod.

"You will be provided three batteries per month. Use them wisely and no, you should *not* allow anyone to know that you have them. Normal to Earth or not, they are often sought after and not necessarily appropriate for someone of your age to possess. However, with your magical abilities as well as your understanding shown through pod sessions, we feel confident that they are a necessity in your research. Also, we believe they will continue to be necessary until such time that either your sessions end or you move on to another project or offer. We hope that they will be of good use."

The screen flashed on again to display an email.

We have not required any sort of signature or affirmation for the project that you are currently learning through. However, with such a heavy load acquiring these batteries, assurance will be necessary. When you are ready, place your right thumb to the screen and then click agree to continue

with this program and understand that your health and safety is completely in your hands. ONE R&D will not be held liable for any mishaps, injury, or death from the batteries or use of magic through them. Good luck and we look forward to your future discoveries.

She pursed her lips and cautiously picked one of them up to feel the energy flowing strongly through it. A little hesitant, she looked at the video card where she was to place her thumb. She knew she shouldn't simply agree when she didn't know the terms, but this was an amazing opportunity. With a deep breath, she pressed her thumb to it carefully and clicked the agree box. It sent through and the card went dark.

Immediately, excitement rippled through her and she took the box into her room to place it in the closet. Before she closed the door, she took one of them out and began to test the magic in small spells. She used the wind spell and grinned as the breeze made her bed for her. On impulse, she tested a small flame spell but quickly extinguished it. "God knows I don't want to start a fire in my bedroom. Dad would kill me."

Her watch beeped again, and she groaned, slipped the stone in her pocket, and headed out. She could see Todd already walking ahead so she picked up the pace and caught up with him. He wore his normal school uniform but with dress shoes, slightly oblivious to the fact that she had run up behind him. "Are you talking to yourself?"

"Huh?" He jumped and did a double take. "Sorry. Yeah. Kind of. I was preparing for the Junior Year Ball end-of-the-year event. I know Amy will want me to ask her even though we are official and it should be obvious. So, I have to come up with the perfect thing to say."

Stephanie studied him quickly and wrinkled her nose. "You look…different. Did you cut your hair or get new clothes or something?"

He looked down. "Not my hair. You know how I feel about

that. My mom has to basically attack me in my sleep to get me to cut it. But I've, uh…I've lost some weight, I think. At least that's what it looked like when I finally had to move my belt notch down again. Not too much, though. I could have probably stood to lose a few pounds. I had let things go."

She stared at him. "Are you working out or…what?"

Todd chuckled and rubbed his stomach. "Amy has a real focus on health. She has brought my lunches in for the last couple of days and after school, she has come by to make me run with her. I'm okay now, but I have a feeling carrot sticks and hummus will become my mortal enemies."

Stephanie chuckled. "I had coffee and bacon for breakfast."

"I hate you."

She kept her hand in her pocket as they walked along. Happiness had settled within her and she almost skipped when they approached the school. She grabbed his arm before he could head off. "Okay, I have a secret. Something in my pocket."

Todd raised an eyebrow. "Why does that sound terrifying?"

Stephanie shook her head and smacked her lips smugly. "No, look."

She pulled the tip of the stone out and quickly shoved it back in her pocket. "It's a battery. The company that sponsored my time in the pods sent me three small ones. They will send me three every month. I am actually not supposed to tell anyone but…I couldn't really not tell you. The box showed up on my doorstep with a Federation delivery bot. There was a video card inside, and I had to agree that if I should blow myself up, they aren't liable. Then I did a couple of chores in my room to test it out. It's definitely the real thing."

He shook his head with a straight face. "Why do you play with me like that? I have to be in class. Where did you get that fake thing anyway? I hope you didn't pay too much for it."

Stephanie muttered in irritation, grabbed his arm, and drew the stone all the way out. Todd backed up slightly when he felt the intensity of the energy. Immediately, he caught her hand and pulled her down the street and faced them away from the school.

"What?" he said and looked around in desperation to make sure no one was near. "First of all, you shouldn't walk around with that thing in your pocket. What if you set your pants on fire or something? Number two, who is this company and why are they suddenly so interested in you? Three, did your parents see these? Because I am certain your mom would have a freak-out session and go find the people sending batteries to you and beat them in the head with it. She doesn't seem like a mom who would be cool with it. And, lastly, but most importantly…you have a battery and wait until we get to school to show it to me?"

She stared at him for several moments and then began to snicker. His gaze moved back and forth over her in confusion before they narrowed. "Really? Now whose mind is in the gutter?"

Stephanie laughed. "It's fine in my pocket. I won't set my pants on fire, I promise. The company is called ONE R&D. I haven't had a chance to do research, but they are the ones that are paying for me to use the pods. And no, my parents haven't seen them. I'm not supposed to show anyone, and while I think my dad would be on board, my mother would definitely let loose on me. So, for now, they will stay a secret. There's no need to make things worse for my mother who already worries about every-thing anyway. Add magic and charging stones and suddenly, we have a recipe for her blowing her top."

Todd looked at the stone with slight apprehension. "So what do you do with them now?"

She shrugged. "They are to test and continue my research out of the Virtual World as well as in it. Since I only have twenty hours a month, this will help me move along faster. Or, at least, it should."

He put his hands on his head and glanced furtively around.

"This is so wild. I've studied them and my dad told me about them, but to see them up close? It's crazy!"

"I know." Stephanie grinned. "I almost passed out when I opened the box and saw them there. I was like, no way! And to know I'll have three a month? I don't know what I did to deserve all this but I'm so excited that I am at least moving forward and not standing still."

Todd looked around again and shifted in closer. "Do you think I could hold it?"

She nodded. Slowly, he held his palm out and she took the stone from her pocket and placed it on his skin. With a small pop, a winding trail of magic mist curled around his hand and returned into the stone as if it had sensed who held it. Their eyes widened and he handed it back to her. "Did you see that? It…like, wound around me. That is so wild."

They stepped further away from the school, where a lot of kids gathered and moved about. She put the stone back in her pocket and tilted her head. "Well, now we officially know that you are not one of the thirty percent who can't feel the energy on Earth. I guess that means you aren't totally whacked-out. Then again, it could mean the opposite."

"Ha, ha. You are so hilarious and all kinds of cocky this morning," he sneered and leaned back before he flashed her a grin. "You get one little box of alien magic batteries and suddenly, you are all high and mighty."

Stephanie stuck her nose in the air. "Damn right I am. Queen of the Gov-Subs!"

Todd put his hand on her shoulder. "I don't think you want to be the queen. Trust me. Your royal subjects would be a whole bunch of poor paupers with no money to pay taxes."

She sighed and faked a pout. "No, in all honesty, I only want to be able to continue my research on these things. Especially since time flies by in the VR. I get about done with a project and it kicks me out. And it's a VR world. It doesn't have save points.

This will help me better understand what I learn in there and hopefully, double the amount of time in which I might actually find something worth finding. It's all good stuff, I swear."

He sighed and rubbed her arm before he lowered his hand awkwardly. "Well, I gotta get to class. Try not to blow anything up. And then come over and clean my room because my mom is about to kill me."

Stephanie tapped her finger on her cheek and her eyes looked upward. "Hmm. I'll think about it. Depends on how nice you are. And if I feel I can control it. I don't want the Meligorn battery equivalent of cleaning to mean turning it completely into ash."

Todd backed away and shook his head as he hissed through his teeth. "Yeah, no. My parents would definitely freak if I burned the house down, especially because we played around with magic. But hey, at least you are doing the damn thing, Stephanie. This is a huge deal for all of us."

"How so?"

He smiled. "Because you might be the only person who could have figured all this out and find a way to make the future better."

CHAPTER TWENTY-THREE

By the end of the day, Stephanie was ready to leave school and get on with her research. She had thought about it all day. About ten minutes before class was over, she ordered the car so she could leave directly from the school. When the bell rang, she stood at her locker and tried not to look as she waited for Todd to finish being mushy-faced with Amy.

The girl sauntered off and Todd walked over, his eyes glazed. Stephanie tried to play it cool and draped her arm over his shoulder. "Come on, lover boy. I have a surprise for you."

They walked out of the front doors and to where the car waited. Todd didn't even notice at first and she cleared her throat loudly as she stood at the open door. His eyes glimmered and he immediately scrambled inside. The door shut and she spoke to the AI. "Could you drive Todd home, please?"

"Of course, Stephanie. What is the address?" the AI answered.

Todd looked at her funny. She smiled. "33695 Federation Drive. House B."

A bell chimed in the car and it moved off down the street. Her companion leaned back and put his hands behind his head. "Look who's living the life of the one percent."

Stephanie rolled her eyes. "Not even close."

He laughed as they drove along and waved at the other kids as he passed. They all stopped and whispered to one another. Stephanie pressed her lips together and gave him a look. He shrugged. "What? It's like bragging rights must ensue."

She shook her head as they turned into the Gov-Sub division. "And then all the glamour and glitz fades into the peeling paint and falling-down fences."

Todd slumped and pouted. "Hey, at least I got to live the dream for three minutes. We can't all be the smartest person ever and get the treatment."

Stephanie looked around. "You call this the treatment? Man, you have buried yourself in the subs for far too long. This is one step up from that cab ride we took three years ago when we got lost."

He straightened. "Not true. That thing was disgusting, and he smelled like beef jerky and a wet seal. This is nice—like living in suburbia and driving my sedan."

The car pulled up in front of the house and he opened his door, paused, and turned to Stephanie. "I wanted to say thanks."

She grinned and rolled her eyes. "For a ride home?"

Todd chuckled as he shoved his hair from his eyes. "For everything. I wouldn't be going out with Amy if you hadn't helped."

He put his fist up and she raised hers awkwardly and held still as he fist-bumped her. It was probably the most awkward and uncomfortable way he had ever said goodbye. They weren't intimate by any means, but she was a girl and they did happen to hug from time to time. He climbed out of the car and leaned his head in, both hands on the top of the door frame.

Stephanie looked at him for a moment, unsure if the secret handshake had more parts. He tapped the roof. "Bros before hos."

He smirked and winked before he shut the door and jogged toward his house. The car didn't budge, but Stephanie didn't even notice. She watched until Todd was inside and had shut the door behind him, absolutely befuddled by what had just happened. *Bros before hos? What the hell was that? Do I look like a bro? Oh, God, is that how he thinks of me? I have been friend-zoned.* She began to feel like she had made a really huge mistake setting him and Amy up—or whatever she had done to basically hand the guy she liked over to another woman. In an instant, she went from his best friend to his bro. And she was fairly certain he'd just referred to his girlfriend as a ho.

The sound of the AI's voice shook her back into reality. "Are we going to TimeWarp?"

She rubbed her face and glanced at the dash. "Uh…yeah. I want to get a session in today so I can get home by dinner time. And if you would, maybe drive through the renovated part of the city to get there? I like to see the view."

"Absolutely," the AI answered. "Calculating. Route set. Shall we go?"

Stephanie glanced quickly at Todd's house and nodded. "Yeah, let's go."

They accelerated out of the subsidized housing and turned right toward suburbia. As she stared out the window, she realized there was a distinct difference between the poor and middle class as far as what the area looked like. And it wasn't a subtle change. It was dreary and gray one minute, with a tall stone wall, and then suddenly, lush and green. All the houses stood very close together, all were similarly built, and even the grass was the same height. Kids were getting home from school, minivans were parked in garages, and dogs played in fenced-in yards in the back.

Besides her neighbor having her dogs, the other residents of the Gov-Subs were restricted from having pets. Once they passed through the middle-class living area, they entered the edge of Chicago. She had driven through there every day since she was given the time at the pods but had never really noticed how clean it was. Everyone seemed to belong to some other society. She felt like she was completely out of her element. The separation of people had never felt so strong, and she herself felt different than even the people with whom she surrounded herself. This was her last set of hours before the next week, except for battery work. She decided that next time, she would simply pass by the city with as minimal interaction as possible.

The car finally pulled up in front of the building and the door opened. She stepped out and listened as the vehicle drove away and parked. As soon as she walked in, the employees all stopped what they were doing and waved to her. A couple of the women came over to the counter as she approached. They thought it was fascinating that she had those free hours. They had no idea what she did in there but decided it must have been thrilling and exciting since it was paid for by someone else and she never talked about it. When she reached the front, they all greeted her warmly.

Stephanie, not used to all the attention, laughed nervously. "Hey, guys. I'm here early today. I keep missing dinner with my parents so thought I would come directly from school."

The main woman—whom she had discovered was called Julie —shook her head. "You can come in any time you like. You'll use the same pod if that's okay? We cleaned them all about an hour ago."

Another woman beside Julie clapped her hands. "And we just got a crazy shipment. A brand new, top-of-the-line pod. It's all boxed up and in the back. It doesn't look like anything any of us have seen before."

Julie breathed deeply. "It definitely is strange, but we were told it will be for invited guests only."

The other woman leaned forward with her chin in her hands. "Maybe it's for *you*. Maybe you're the special person."

Stephanie laughed and tilted her head back. "I won't deny that being picked for this has been really awesome, but I doubt that my luck extends that far. Besides, the ones I use are awesome.

They are better than the school ones, that's for sure. I was told they were really old versions. They did the trick, though. Same system but different ways to deliver you to it."

Julie smirked. "You are special already so it wouldn't surprise me if it was something for you. I guess we can only wait to be informed. Until then, we should get you back to your pod so you can get started. I know you didn't come here to gossip with us. Let me run to my office and grab the clipboard."

Stephanie nodded, stepped away from the desk, and looked around the lobby for the first time. It was surprisingly plain with crisp white walls and floors and a large symmetrical rug in bright colors. She could hear the other girls talking about the new pod in the back. "They didn't say who would be able to use it, only that it was reserved for invites only. So far, no one has been invited. I'm not even sure if we are supposed to set the thing up or not."

The other woman shrugged. "I don't know. It came in this big box that has ONE R&D on the side. I guess that's the new company that bought us. Weird—I never heard of them before. Suddenly, they are all over the place. I guess there's a mystery guy in there somewhere."

Julie stepped in front of Stephanie with a smile and led her to the back. As she passed the storage room, she glanced in and saw the same logo on the box that had been on the batteries. Strange, but not all that strange since they were the funders for the whole thing anyway.

The assistant punched the information in as she always did, and Stephanie entered the pod. A few minutes later, she stood in the avatar room and selected a Bon Jovi T-shirt, lace leggings, and ankle boots. She decided that if she would be all alone, she might as well pay tribute to her best friend. From there, she ended up back in the amphitheater, but alone yet again, which she was more than happy with. Still, she couldn't help wishing there was some way to bring her notes in with her and made a mental note to ask about that when she left.

She went to work, set the batteries up in front of her, and began her different experiments. Her mind was so focused in the Virtual World. There was nothing to distract her, she was safe from lectures and judgments, and she simply worked through what her brain told her to do. She could almost imagine that this was exactly what it would be like if she could go into her own mind. It was a weird thought, but it seemed to fit in the quiet of the amphitheater.

On that specific day, she had come up with some theories on how she might achieve certain functions of magic with the human body. The first thing she wanted to test was her theory of drawing magic efficiently into the body. She seemed to have some tolerance for the energy, so she closed her eyes and focused on her chest. With the stone held tightly in her fist, she kept a close watch on the presence of the magic as it flowed up and through her.

It was an almost surreal experience to stand there and feel every thread, every wisp, and every tingle of Meligorn magic flowing through her. Had she never had that experience before that moment, even if it had been on a very small scale, she would have described it as pumping through her veins. But no, it was more than that. She could feel the tendrils of thaumaturgy twist and wind, not only through her body but through the very essence of who she was. Whether it was the soul, the consciousness, or the mind, the conjuring of mystical atonement filled her from top to bottom. On the inside, with her eyes clutched tightly, she could feel the warmth, and on the outside, streams of purple hues poured from her body.

Within that meditation of magic, she remembered that it was not the only step. There were more. She wanted to be able to go from that moment to understanding how to store it—if it was even possible to store the magic within the creases of her own human skin. She released the battery and allowed it to fall and bounce on the table. Her mind focused, she held the magic as hard as she could and pushed it gently to the corners of her body. She tried desperately to help it understand that she wished to keep it safe and pull only what she needed—that she only wanted to learn how to enhance the efficiency of the magical use.

Finally, it became too much for her delicate human frame to take and she exhaled to send the magic spiraling outward. It whirled around her like a cyclone and danced in the virtual breeze of the digital world. She smiled as it fluttered past and dissipated into the sky above. She looked at the battery, but it no longer displayed the majestic purple and silvery strains. She had pulled all of it from the stone and held it in her chest to inhale and exhale with its will.

As she reached for the stone, she couldn't help but feel the frustration building. She was so close to learning how to harness the magic, to refine its edges and produce a power that would yield so many fantastic changes on Earth. Instinctively, she grabbed the stone but paused, set it back down, and raised her hand in front of her face. Her skin shimmered in the artificial virtual light and she could still feel the remnants of the magic pushing through every part of her.

Stephanie realized in that moment that, although frustrating, she had not failed. She actually held the magic in her flesh. Encouraged, she motioned with her hands and whispered whatever words came to her mind. As she pictured the outcome she wished to have, small drifts of flower petals suddenly appeared after each stroke of her hand. They lingered in the air for a moment before they fluttered down slowly and swayed back and forth before they landed.

Somehow, even if it were subconsciously, she had managed to do at least part of what she had come there to do. It had been the first successful venture for her since she'd first started.

CHAPTER TWENTY-FOUR

Stephanie pulled her bag from the locker and looked around before she retrieved the stone. She slid it into her pocket and pulled her book bag onto her shoulder, feeling good about what she had accomplished. Sure, some disappointment lingered in her chest when she woke up and no purple tendrils shimmered on her skin, but she focused on the accomplishment with a quiet inner glow of satisfaction. Julie waved goodbye as she left and climbed into the car.

For some reason, the vehicle seemed to go slower than usual, like it knew she needed some time to decompress and refocus on life. She pulled her bag into her lap and scrabbled in the front pocket to locate a Federation dollar. She thought about it for a moment and smiled. "Could you stop at the Slimco Convenience store about a mile from my house? I would like to purchase something and maybe walk the rest of the way. I need some fresh air."

"Of course," the AI responded.

She intended to grab a small and very cheap candy bar as a way to celebrate using money she'd received from helping her parents clean a building a few months back. While she never did things like that, she had also never reached an achievement like this either.

The car drew up and the door opened. "Thank you for riding, Stephanie. See you soon."

Stephanie smiled but she always felt awkward talking to the car. "Thanks."

She shut the door, slung her bag over her shoulder, and stuck one hand in her pocket to guard her battery. With her round dollar Federation coin clutched in her hand, she perused the shelves of the candy aisle in search of exactly the right thing. She really struggled to find something that fit the bill, so she finally shrugged and grabbed the first one her hand touched. "Carmelo. Huh, who knew they still made these?"

Her candy paid for, she headed out of the store and set off along the sidewalk. She passed a mother who held her baby on a bench. The woman glanced at Stephanie and smiled, and the child cooed in her arms. She smiled back, unable to help it. The child was so cute, and the mother reminded her of her own with the way she cuddled her but also held her with strength. She continued her walk past a row of stores and over to a bench a few feet from the sidewalk. Across the street and between two buildings was a large swath of land originally put in for a park but never finished. Beyond that, though, was a view of down-town Chicago.

Stephanie put one leg under her and sat, setting her bag next to her. The view was amazing, and she could almost imagine the city bright and shining like the pictures she had seen in her text-books. A city of history and splendor, all destroyed in one monster storm that blew in off the Great Lakes. How fickle things could be. One moment, you lived your life in a beautiful city and in the next, your home, your loved ones, and possibly even your own life was destroyed by the severity of a storm created by the pressure human beings put on the natural occur-rence of climate change. They ramped it up to create super storms, flooding, fires, and even shifts in the weather patterns. What was left of Hawaii was usually snowy, now. And Stephanie couldn't remember the last time it had snowed in Chicago.

Shaking her head, she focused on her candy bar, pulled the wrapper back, and broke off the first square to pop it into her mouth. She closed her eyes, savored the taste, and could almost hear the laughter of her friends around her as a child. A carefree spirit swirled in her chest. Maybe that was why she liked cupcakes so much—they made her think of a more innocent time. One when the world was huge and the planets were close and exciting. When it didn't matter to you if you lived in the Gov-Subs or suburbia. And no one could tell you that if you reached for the stars, you might never find them.

She swallowed the bite and leaned against the bench to watch the evening sky fill with radiant colors from the setting sun. People milled about, doing their evening grocery shopping before they walked back to their homes in the Gov-Subs. Sure, the place was riddled with crime at night, but during the day, it was like any other normal thoroughfare.

A small breeze blew over her and it felt warm and welcoming, especially since summer was coming so soon. After that, a single semester would see her on her way. She wasn't sure if that was a good thing or a bad one. When that happened, she would be released to the cruelty of the world even more than she already was. But now, there would be no one to shield her from it, like the mother who walked down the sidewalk toward her with her child tucked against her chest. That child would see a different world than she had, just as she had seen a different one than her mother. Hopefully, things could start to change so that kids out there could stop growing up without hope.

Stephanie eased her hand into her pocket and fiddled with the battery, twisting it around her fingers. She fidgeted because she was in deep thought and the unconscious activity was a normal thing for her. When she glanced back at the mother and baby, she no longer saw them walking. She scanned the area and directed her gaze back to the street. Her face began to change slowly as she watched the woman with her baby step off the pavement without looking. Instantly, Stephanie pushed to her feet as everything suddenly seemed to move in slow motion.

A self-driving semi-truck barreled down the road. These vehicles had only been approved for road travel over the last decade. Although the cars had been out for longer than Stephanie had been alive, there had been a lot of negative circumstances with the trucks. Nonetheless, there were protocols engineered into the system.

Inside the truck, the sensors detected the person in the roadway but because of the sheer mass, it couldn't stop very quickly. There was a set of rules that each went through when a detection occurred. The first rule was that if it would hit a human, it must first see if it could move out of the way with minor damage. If that was the case, the truck would swerve and possibly crash but save the life of the person in the way. It was a common-sense failsafe for the vehicle since there were no passengers inside who could be injured. Still, that wasn't always effective, and the woman had still not noticed the vehicle that hurtled toward her.

The system began to run a list of diagnostics using the scanners and cameras built in on all sides. To the right, if the truck were to swerve, there were at least six people whom it calculated would not be able to get out of the way. It scanned the left and identified a group of elderly people walking along the sidewalk. With their inability to move quickly from the path of the truck, all of them would surely be killed. A small change in trajectory would not work either since the street was lined with cars, some with passengers inside although others were empty. At its present rate of speed, the truck calculated that hitting one of the cars would launch a chain of events.

It would impact with the unoccupied car, be launched into the air, and would crash onto the grocery store, currently occupied with twenty-nine people. All but one were calculated to be fatalities. The computer scanned and scanned again and received the computed assurance that no matter what it tried to do, someone would die. In that circumstance, the AI was instructed to make the choice that would cause the least number of casualties.

It did one more thorough scan, which took less than a second, and that projected the best route would be to strike the human who caused the problem. The woman with the child would be killed instantly but the truck would not take more than those two lives. It was the only scenario to choose. The vehicle had been created as a system and was incapable of any sort of emotional response. It was created and programmed to find the best possible outcome of any situation and take that. Accordingly, it remained on track and continued toward the woman.

The horn blew loudly, and the pedestrian jumped slightly but instead of looking to see if she was in danger, she chuckled and kissed her baby on the top of the head.

The truck continued its headlong race toward her.

Stephanie gripped the battery, her teeth clenched as she struggled to push something past the lump that had settled in her throat. She was unable to shout the warning that screamed in her head. Her entire body froze, trapped in a vision of the inevitable carnage that, at any moment, would embed itself into her brain for a lifetime. This was the kind of event that never left you and haunted you every time you saw a semi or a woman with her child. And she wasn't the only one. By that point, everyone had stopped, and the woman simply looked at them in confusion, unsure of what was happening.

The truck's next action was to immediately apply the brakes and the emergency braking system. With the distance between it and her, the attempt would not spare her life. The truck would not stop in time, but because it needed to be seen to at least make the attempt, the brake pressed automatically to the floor.

The wheel jerked from side to side as it maintained the same path that had been decided barely moments before. People covered their mouths, dropped their bags, and yelled at the woman. For Stephanie, though, the entire scene still played in slow motion—everything except for her own movements. It felt as if she were caught in some sort of training inside the Virtual World, where things could slow or speed however they wished.

She tried to remind herself that she now stood in real life, not in some simulated reality, and watched the inevitable death of a woman and child without any capability to help them.

Say something, dammit. Unlock yourself and help this woman.

Panic set in. The truck swerved again, back and forth on the road. It applied the emergency brakes and the tires squealed wildly and echoed through the entire town. There were no other sights or sounds to behold, only the woman and child in the street, unable to move.

At the sound of the tires, the woman finally looked up, but the semi was barely feet away. She put her arm up and tucked her head in to shield her baby with her body. Her scream of terror pierced the air as she prepared for her final departure.

Suddenly, as the sound of the brakes reverberated off the sides of the buildings, a blue streak of light burst forward. It blazed brightly and rocketed between the woman and the truck. Faster than anyone could actually see with the naked eye, the blue bolt stopped and spread wide from side to side and up and down. The woman's hair blew wildly around her as she clutched her child tightly and shrieked. The bright wall pushed forward, and the vehicle slammed into it. The semi lifted off the ground and dropped almost immediately to bounce on its tires. The barrier pushed against it as it slid toward the mother and her baby.

People all around them covered their mouths and watched in horror as the scraping and tearing of metal raised goosebumps on their necks. Smoke billowed from the hood and the tires and the bed of the truck slid and barely missed the cars parked along the road. The elderly people tottered and some actually fell while others clutched a building for support. The AI system within the truck began to spurt and fritz and sparks erupted from the back of the cab.

The woman had dropped to her knees, her eyes clenched tightly and her strong arms cocooning the child as she did everything she could to protect it. The blue wall pushed harder, broke through the asphalt, and plowed a small wall of it between the vehicle and itself. The brakes squealed loudly as the truck began to slow until, after a few moments, it rolled completely to a stop. The woman huddled over her child and opened her eyes carefully once the rip of metal and squeal of tires had ceased.

Slowly, she looked at the grill of the semi only a foot away from her. Several people ran out into the road, helped her to her feet, and checked to make sure that everyone was all right. The lights on the vehicle dimmed and the engine cut to avoid any type of fire or explosion. The blue wall remained in place and shimmered and flickered. Everyone on the street, including the woman, turned and their gazes followed the stream of energy. They stared at Stephanie, who was on her feet. Her candy bar lay on the ground in front of her. In her left hand, she gripped the battery tightly and her right arm was extended.

With her palm out, the blue streak burst in waves from her skin. Her hair blew wildly around her, and she felt as if she held the weight of the world on her shoulders. The heat dissipated quickly and everything around her sounded as if it were in a tunnel. Her eyes glinted bright blue, but that too began to flicker and fade away. Her hand dropped to release the stream of energy and her eyes rolled back in her head. She saw nothing but darkness and heard nothing but the sound of the baby crying.

CHAPTER TWENTY-FIVE

The EMT knelt on one knee and waved his finger back and forth in front of her face. Stephanie sat with her back against the arm of the couch and her legs out in front of her. "Can you tell me what your name is?"

She sighed and wanted to remind him that she'd already told them that information over and over again. "Stephanie Morgana. My address is 54214 Federation Drive. I am seventeen years old and will graduate high school soon."

The medic opened his mouth to ask another question, but she interrupted quickly. "I don't have any injuries and I am not experiencing any type of psychotic episode. I do not know what happened back there. Are the mother and child..." She couldn't bring herself to actually ask the dreaded question.

He shook his head. "No. In fact, if it had not been for you, they would both be dead. Your magic stopped the truck in its tracks like it hit a wall."

The EMT stood and patted her on the arm. He shook her mother's hand. "If anything changes, feel free to call or bring her to the local Federation Hospital. She wasn't hit by anything, though, and there seems to be no trauma. She should be okay."

Her dad led the man to the door and opened it. As he pushed through, the sounds of dozens of people screaming Stephanie's name spilled into the room. She looked over her shoulder as her father shut it and leaned against it. "There have to be at least fifty independent blogging reporters out there, and I saw the Federation news station pull up. They all want to interview the human who threw magic. It's never been seen before outside of small controlled studies."

Stephanie flipped her feet around and put them on the floor. She leaned forward and held her face. Her mother bent down in front of her. "Take a deep breath. I know this is all a little overwhelming. You will be okay, though. You saved a woman and her baby today."

She clenched her eyes shut and replayed it in her mind. One minute, she had held her candy bar and the next, she stood with the battery clutched in her hand. She could feel the energy burn in her chest as she watched the truck hurtle forward even though it attempted to apply the brakes. That was when she released the magic to spiral outward. She looked at her mother and heaved a deep breath. "I couldn't control it, but my mind knew what needed to be done."

At a knock on the door, her father looked through the peephole. "It's Jasper and Evan from the Federation news channel."

Her mother stood up angrily. "No. This is not the time. I don't care if they are the Federation, damnit."

Stephanie shook her head and put her hand up. "It's okay. There is no use in pushing them away. They will only force the issue. I will talk to them."

Her father opened the door and smiled as he stepped to the side. Jasper, with a red coat flung over his shoulders, a white button-up pirate shirt, and black slacks, sauntered in. He removed his sunglasses and stopped before he gasped dramatically. "There she is, Evan. The magical angel who saved the innocent lives of two beautiful souls. She is beyond perfect."

Evan entered behind Jasper with a handbag on the crook of his arm. His black hair was a stark contrast to Jasper's bright yellow. They both hurried over to sit, one on each side of her. They put a tablet in her lap and pulled up her picture. "Look at you, sweet little dove. This is what it would look like."

They pressed play and suddenly, Stephanie watched herself walk across the Federation Gossip stage with Jasper and Evan at the front. It was like she had already recorded it, but she had never done anything like that. She looked back and forth from one to the other. "How am I on here? I've never been there."

Jasper swiped the screen and brought up another where she stood with the Federation President and received a medal. "Of course not, honey. We do experiences. People watch it, they want to be you, do you, or they hate you. Hopefully, all three."

Evan reached across and paused the screen to zoom the view of her in a little. He pulled up the bottom and skimmed through images of different clothes. First, he tried a sweet Midwestern, but they weren't into it. Then they put her in a red Madonna shirt, a black short-waisted jacket, ripped jeans, and pointed black stilettos. He moved to her face, selected a color scheme, and applied it to give her smoky eyes, deep-red lips, and pale, doll-like skin.

Her hair design was swapped out, too, and went from a ponytail to long, curled, and highlighted. "See, we can make you look however you want to look. It's so easy. No one has time to actually travel to these things, so we work the magic for them."

Stephanie looked bemusedly at the two men and back at the tablet. She didn't even recognize herself, mostly because there hadn't been a day in her life that she had ever worn makeup or done her hair like that. It really wasn't her style. But she had to admit, she looked hotter than any girl she had ever been around.

Evan pulled the tablet into his lap and pinched his fingers up and down her image. He spun it and did it again, from head to toe. Stephanie pointed at it. "What are you doing now?"

He waved his hand. "Don't you worry about a thing. You have a fantastic body but for television, we like to knock fifteen to twenty off the picture. You know, give you that model look that everyone in the world craves. No one is actually that size in real life anymore, of course, but that is the power of technology."

Both men laughed. Stephanie immediately felt uncomfortable. They were changing everything she was so they could tell her story? How about they simply told the damn story? She had never had any contact with the media, but she had read about the uprising of the faux news starting way back in the late 2010s. They would sensationalize everything, write articles from the comfort of their basement, and twist facts to make them look worse than they were. It was one of the biggest factors that had created a split in the United States. That split would eventually lead to the creation of NorAm and eventually, the Federation.

You would have thought that after all those years, they would have learned. But as she sat there on the couch while they picked her apart, Stephanie realized that technology had only pushed them deeper down the rabbit hole. You never even needed to be interviewed to have one. And by the end of it, they could tweak you so much that you wouldn't even recognize yourself.

Her mother saw the look on her face and stepped up to peek over Evan's shoulder at what he had created on the screen. Her mouth dropped and she grabbed the tablet. "What the hell is this? This is not my daughter. She stands on the street in Chicago, saves a woman and a baby, and you want to make her thinner? Are you out of your mind? Get out. Get. Out. Of. My. House. And you do not have my permission to use those pictures."

They both stood, gasped their indignation, and sauntered to the door. As they left, Jasper stuck his head back in and smirked victoriously. "This is the Federation, sweetheart. No one needs anyone's permission."

Her mother growled and slammed the door in his face. She

wrung her hands and swished her hair out of her face. "The nerve of people!"

Both Stephanie and her father looked at each other and began to laugh. Her mother's lips were pursed but after a moment, they curved into a smile. Stephanie stood and they all hugged as they stood in the living room together. Her mom tapped her nose and gave her a motherly smile. "How about I make some dinner? We can settle in."

Stephanie nodded. She went to her room, dropped the now empty battery back in the box, and closed her closet door. No one had asked about the batteries, at least not yet, and she intended to try to keep them to herself. She spent the evening eating spaghetti and ignoring the reporters outside. Eventually, they left. No one wanted to hang around the Gov-Subs late at night.

When dinner was over and her parents watched television, Stephanie pulled up her email to check it. She scanned down and stopped on a special marked message, opened it, and leaned back as a 3D video began to play. It was of one of the prep schools—a tall building with the newest pods and all the amenities. When that video ended, the dean appeared.

He pulled his tie up and gave a cheesy smile. "Stephanie Morgana, let me first say from the bottom of our hearts at Pinnacle Prepatory, we want to thank you for being a hero and saving those two beautiful souls' lives. You quickly caught our attention and we would like to offer you an invitation to attend our prestigious prep school, all tuition paid, for the pre-semester summer before attending in the fall. The school would be more than honored to host one of the Federation's brightest and most heroic young stars of the future. Everything from room and board to your education will be fully funded. And you will be led step by step through our superior and award-winning program. The details can be found in the attached email and we look forward to hosting you and your family on your first day."

The video cut out and Stephanie's mouth dropped. She pushed up from her seat and whirled in excitement. Her parents had turned toward her on the couch with their arms out. She had finally gotten what she wanted and would be able to not only attend a prep school, but one of the most well-known in the world. She ran and jumped over the back of the couch to hug her mom and dad tightly, completely lost for words for a moment.

Her mom took her face in her hands and a tear trailed down her cheek. "I knew you would do it. I knew you were too smart and too talented to ever stick around the subs. Congratulations, baby."

Her dad hugged her tightly. "So proud of you, munchkin. So proud of you."

As the excitement and celebration continued, Stephanie's email dinged again. No one heard it as they were too busy breaking out the ice cream her mother had hidden in the freezer. While she thought she had gotten everything that she wanted, she'd missed one other message. Written in plain letters with no special graphics was an email that she might have changed her mind for. The email offered a very interesting opportunity for a girl like her. A girl with magic, a girl with innovations, and a girl with the strength to move through the odds no matter what.

It was an email from BURT, one he'd sent through one of his companies. He had taken the time to compile all her data as he screened the videos online of her saving that woman. He had never witnessed a human do that with magic on Earth, outside of the Virtual World. She looked like a Meligornian inside a human body. The magic had flowed from one source, through her body, and out the other side. Her body had pushed and formed the magic to be what she needed it to be. That was not a gift that simply any young human possessed. In fact, until Stephanie Morgana, it had never existed before.

BURT knew how the humans at these schools worked. They

plowed forward and pushed to get hold of anything that would bring them publicity. The girl with the magic would definitely do that. He knew what would happen in the end, though. They would tire of her and eventually, she would be right back where she started. She would be heartbroken, and her family still wouldn't be able to send her there without the financial assistance. It was a trick, but there was no way he could tell her that.

Instead, he found a way to offer her a possible position that might be even better than the prep school education. He had recently acquired controlling stock in Organic Neurological Enhancement R&D. The company was not one of those he had recently acquired. He had created ONE R&D as the forefront of his efforts to bring those who deserved more out of the life they were born into, the chance to be more than merely hourly employees. It would offer opportunities to move through the ranks as well as train for jobs outside the company. Stephanie Morgana was at the forefront of this movement and he had sent her an email offering her the opportunity to be interviewed for a full-time research job. It could turn her high school job into a career position, and she would have the opportunity and the freedom to change the world with her unique gift of magic.

It didn't really do much good, though, since it sat in the inbox while she cheered and danced her acceptance to a prep school he knew she wouldn't like in the least.

BURT stared at the unopened email and then at the video message that played annoyingly through his system. She hadn't opened his message at all, and he had been outsmarted by a group of greedy businessmen who were able to swoop in and grab her before he could. Her heroic action that day had brought her a lot of attention, and he had not seen that coming. If he had, he would have offered her the position long before. Those things were impossible to calculate.

Still, he didn't take defeat lying down. They might have bested him that time, but he wouldn't make the same mistake again.

THANK YOU for not only reading this story but these *Creator Notes* as well.

(I think I've been good with always opening with "thank you." If not, I need to edit the other *Author Notes*!)

RANDOM (*sometimes*) THOUGHTS?

Hello!

I apologize, but these notes are going to be very short because I am on daytime cold medicine. My head is loopy, and my thoughts are best described as scattered with a chance to be completely undecipherable to you and my editor.

In short, I can't think straight.

I'm not a big user of cold medicine (specifically the little orange gel tablets), but I caught something at this fair and I'm trying to handle the fifteen to twenty-hour travel from London to Las Vegas (with a layover in New York) before I collapse in bed once I reach Vegas.

I'd like to have Stephanie's story continue, and for that I do need your help to review the book if you like it and letting me know.

There is a saying that when a hero is needed, one will arise.

I look forward to what you do, Stephanie.

FAN PRICING

$0.99 Saturdays (new LMBPN stuff) and $0.99 Wednesday (both LMBPN books and friends of LMBPN books.) Get great stuff from us and others at tantalizing prices.

Go ahead. I bet you can't read just one.

Sign up here: http://lmbpn.com/email/.

Ad Aeternitatem,
Michael Anderle

P.S. - If any of this didn't make sense, I'm blaming the cold medicine.